Seraphina Madsen was born in San Rafael, California and grew up on both the East and West Coasts of the United States. She taught English in France for four years and has lived in Germany, The Netherlands, and Sweden. She received an MA in Creative Writing from Kingston University, London. She resides in the UK.

First published in 2016
by Dodo Ink, an imprint of
Dodo Publishing Co Ltd
Flat 5, 21 Silverlands, Buxton SK17 6QH
www.dodoink.com

The right of Seraphina Madsen to be identified as the author of
this work has been asserted in accordance with Section 77 of the
Copyright, Designs and Patents Act 1988

Extract from *On the Road* by Jack Kerouac reprinted by permission of
Penguin Random House Ltd.

This is a work of fiction. Names, characters, places and incidents are
either the product of the author's imagination or are used fictitiously,
and any resemblance to actual persons, living or dead, or actual events
or locales is entirely coincidental.

A CIP record for this book is available from the British Library

Cover design: Dan Stiles
Copy-editor: Jayne White
Proofreader: Dan Coxon
Typesetter: Ben Ottridge

ISBN 978-0-9935758-0-8 paperback

Printed and bound in Great Britain by TJ International,
Trecerus Industrial Estate, Padstow, Cornwall PL28 8RW.

DODGE AND BURN

~~SERAPHINA MADSEN~~

[signature]

*This book
is for Ariel.*

Hunt for American Heiress Continues with Manuscript
Found in Cave in Altamira, Spain
By ALICE SHIFT 7:00 AM ET

A notebook bearing a manuscript and the fingerprints of
Eugenie Lund, an American heiress missing since August
19--, has been found in a cave in Altamira, Spain. Dr
Erik Lund, Antarctic explorer and heir to the publishing
empire established by his late father, has offered a $2m
reward for any information leading to the safe return of his
daughter. The notebook was found by a tourist visiting the
famous Palaeolithic cave paintings, two hundred metres
from its entrance. No further information regarding Lund's
disappearance has surfaced. Below is an excerpt from the
manuscript found inside the notebook.

We were told that our mother's life was terminated by
an attack of killer bees while vacationing in San Marcos,
Mexico, with Dr Vargas at his family home. Vargas described
how the insects had gone for the insides of her ears – a
deliberate technique to destabilise the victim. Mother fell
off the horse, waving her hands in the air to beat them

off and hit her head on a rock. Vargas thought it more prudent to spring the brutal truth upon us rather than the fiction of a prolonged stay in a Mexican hospital followed by eventual death. He bent down close to our faces with a pained expression, miming the scene – mother inert on the ground, Vargas swatting his way through the lethal cloud of throbbing insects, his eventual defeat as he was heavily bombarded in a kamikaze-esque onslaught he likened to the attack of the USS Bunker Hill. All the way through this pantomime, a small shifty spot in his account brushed my brow like the wing of a bat. Vargas assured us mother was unconscious and had not suffered. The killer bee specialists informed him that the perfume she was wearing (Fleurissimo, commissioned by Prince Rainier III for Grace Kelly composed of tuberose, Bulgarian rose, violet, and Florentine iris) had incited the bees to violence. If she and Dr Vargas had been smoking cigarettes, the attack would never have happened. Killer bees abhor smoke, even from one cigarette.

Our father was in the midst of an expedition to Antarctica and could not be found. Dr Vargas adopted us – in accordance with our mother's will, in the event of her death and the inability to locate any kin. The adoption process was quick in light of the fact it took place in Mexico. We ceased to be Lunds and became Vargases.

We moved shortly thereafter, with our beloved Great Danes, Viktor and Shiloh, from Mexico to the coast of Maine with bruise-coloured squalls, milky blizzards, crystallised winter wonderlands and picturesque summers. The house in the forest reminded us of the Russian fairy tales and Tolkien epics our mother and father used to read to us at bedtime. For the first few weeks we wondered whether we had been swooped up into the hinterlands of Siberia but the fantasy was dispelled when Vargas took us for a drive into the Arcadian mountains where, along the way, we passed rambling farm houses, mobile homes, mongrel capes and ranches, all with American flags flying on the front lawns, along with a proliferation of various lawn ornaments — windmills, geese, deer, flamingos, gnomes, the occasional exposed buttocks in the form of a painted wood cut-out meant to resemble a person bending over, for those who wished to turn their lawn into a smutty joke.

The first two years we remained in hiding, confined to the house and grounds. The great rambling Queen Anne edifice was concealed in the forest – elaborate and irregular, made of stone and wood with numerous towers, turrets, verandas, gables and dormers adorned with patterned shingle roofs. Vargas had reason to believe we were at risk of being kidnapped. For this, there were also armed men the Doctor brought from his home town in Mexico who patrolled the area and lived in huts we were forbidden to approach. We were of course not to have any communications with them whatsoever, not even pantomimes. A regimented life began. We quickly apprehended that a surface obedience must be maintained, or else suffer the consequences.

In spring, Camille and I collected flowers to make tea in the forest behind the house. After checking the rabbit snares we would follow a path to a break in the canopy of trees where white, lace-like flower formations fanned out, seeming from a distance to hover in the air. The plant's stalks were mottled an enchanting blood red and in the colour there was a message. It became immediately apparent to us both that the plant had been placed there by forest spirits to turn humans into faeries. If we could transform ourselves, we would be free. Then we could find father. Surely his love for us was so great that our change in form would be of no consequence. In fact, it was quite likely he would be impressed by our feat. We made a tea with the leaves, flowers and stalks and christened it Pan's Elixir. To our great surprise, nothing happened. There was no discernible change in us or our environment. Then it dawned on Camille that the plant alone had little or no effect, perhaps because it was meant to be used in an alchemy with other plants, rituals, or spells we had yet to find, but which would be revealed to us in time. There was also the possibility the potion had a cumulative effect. We decided to continue drinking the elixir, in the hope that its power would eventually come alive in us.

If we were lucky, four rabbits would be caught in the snares. We rubbed pine pitch on our hands before skinning them. A knife was never necessary. You can just tear their hides off. It's like they're wearing a snowsuit. In torrential downpours we gutted them in the shed. It was cleaner to do the skinning and gutting outside. In the snow was best, on a clear day under the ice-encrusted canopies with the sun coming through. The guts are easily jiggled out onto the ground once the rabbit is cut open and best left for an animal to eat. We tied the skinned, hollowed rabbits around tree branches straight as effigy poles and carried them home, pink in the sun along with handfuls of the Pan Elixir flowers.

Some days, before checking the snares, we would walk through the forest to higher ground where underneath the eighty-foot pines stood a small cabin. Curiosity and the thrill of exploration had driven us there. The first time we set eyes on the scene it reminded us of Gustav Doré's etchings, wreathing and humming, flickering before us with the darkness and light of fairy tales. Camille's cheeks flushed. I felt the throb of her exhilaration and surprise, her wide eyes darting into mine as we made our approach through beams of sun and twisting, cool shadows, until we reached the front wooden steps where Camille grinned impishly, batting off the gnats, mosquitoes and other flying insects. I knocked on the door. Then we found a crowbar in a shed and popped a window open.

This cabin became our church. We made an altar, burned sage and performed ceremonies consistent with accounts of the Passamaquoddy tribe described in a social anthropological study we had found in one of the vast libraries nestled inside of the magnificent and terrifying Queen Anne mansion house that had been our mother's family home. We had access to two of the libraries and suspected a third behind one of the great, locked walnut doors on the fourth floor. It was our hope that the knowledge contained within these rooms would aid us in plotting, conniving and fighting our way out of that hell. Sometimes we came upon notes in the front pages and margins of the books that we supposed were in our mother's or father's handwriting and made collections of them in our respective rooms, praying all the while that Dr V did not find out. Of course he did, and locked them in the one library forbidden to us. We read voraciously, four or five books at a time, and compiled notebooks with our theories and findings.

Inside a study of Midwestern Native North American tribes was an inscription in black ink in our father's fluid scrawl, a pseudo-haiku poem he had written for our mother:

Two fawns in the wood,

A fire rages,

I would kill for your love.

(It was unsettling.)

According to our maps the Passamaquoddy reservation was a twenty-minute drive away but Vargas never took us there, despite our pleas. He said that the foray would only lead to disappointment as the natives were hostile to white people on their land. We had to make do with the books in the library.

Along with Native American rites we delved into other sources of ancient knowledge from around the world. We prayed to the Great Spirit, to pantheons of gods and goddesses, to the ancestors, making a plea for Dr Vargas's deliverance from earthly incarnation into a death not even the Ba or Ka could survive – a total annihilation of his soul and essence. In return we offered ourselves as sacrifices, in the service of those legions of supernatural beings to whom we prayed for protection, signs and direction.

Camille and I often smoked sage in a pipe we'd found in the cabin. One day we had a vision. There was a man. He walked around the room but he didn't pace. Everything he did, he did with purpose – there was intelligence behind it. He spent a long time cleaning guns. He looked sad and kind. After he had left we could still smell his spice-scented aftershave and gun oil. We suspected he was the ghostly double (*vardøger* in Norse mythology) who precedes a living person, performing their actions in advance. We weren't ever surprised to see the man's spectral form pass through the cabin door with his dog behind him, or to find him anywhere in the vicinity of the pine forest that contained the cabin, for that matter. His presence elicited mixed feelings of angst and attraction. Each time he appeared it was as though a spell was cast. We would go dizzy for a moment and all would seem as though something had shifted, but we could not pinpoint what exactly. In this altered state was the certainty that our destiny was linked to this man's, that our paths would cross and that he was, for us, some kind of a saviour. (This knowledge did not stop us from trying to save ourselves, however – we continued with the Pan's Elixir tea, ancient rites, occult practices, et cetera.)

The man stayed with us for minutes or even hours. His image would flicker, like a TV screen on the fritz, then return to full force, inevitably flickering out again at the end of the transmission. We knew the dog's name was Brigitte because on several occasions we had heard the man's phantom call to her echoing off the boulders through the wood. But the man did not speak clearly otherwise and we did not learn his name. In the beginning we referred to him simply as The Man. At one point we thought he should be called The Hermit, but it seemed to us he was not truly that. He appeared to be searching for something – a memory, something inside his head. We toyed with The Seeker, but that was not right either.

One afternoon we had the occasion to follow him and Brigitte on one of their hunts and came up with a name that stuck. When the flickering phantasm of the deer came into sight he stopped dead in his tracks with Brigitte not five feet from him and slowly raised the rifle. The buck stood frozen through the trees at a good distance, perhaps five hundred years away. Before the animal could turn its head and bound off in the opposite direction, it fell with the crack of the rifle blast. The man was very good, an expert. From that day forward we called him Deadeye. We longed for the day we would meet him in the flesh.

In our cabin we discovered that time was not as immutable as Dr Vargas had led us to believe. He used this illusory 'fourth dimension', among other things, to contain us but one day we came upon a passage in a study of Africa which supported our own observations and empowered us. According to the author, the inhabitants of Africa believed time to be a creation of man which the gods and ancestors had consented to allow into being. It had a yielding and compliant nature and could vanish, only to reappear with alternating shapes, courses, and rhythms. This was so because its very existence depended on men and woman directing their energy toward it. When time is neglected, it disappears. Camille used to say the same of the deities, and was also quick to point out that even physics textbooks confirmed the fact that time's rate of passage varies in perception, and also in reality, quite dramatically even, as one approaches the speed of light.

For example, if a group of people were to travel in a rocket at ninety-nine percent the speed of light and orbit the Earth for ten years, upon their return they would find that seventy years had passed down below. Because of the speed at which they were travelling, these rocketeers would have aged only ten years while everyone else left behind on Earth had aged seventy. Dr Vargas spent the many years of our captivity devoted to experiments which aimed to break the mechanism of time on earth. He used us as his subjects, as was the case for all of his investigations into the natural world. Vargas told us that if it were possible to travel the speed of light, one would be everywhere in the cosmos all at once. He said there was evidence to suggest that what we know as time is happening all at once, with all moments of one's life accessible at any given point or node. Our biology creates the illusion that it is happening chronologically.

Camille and I applied the knowledge we'd gleaned from Dr Vargas's teachings to some of our own. Like this we were often able to steal time from Vargas, reaching states in which the minutes became hours. We sensed when it was time to leave – Vargas had a palpable psychic radar he had acquired in India that would eventually find us like a heat-seeking missile – a chill spooled up our spines and our palms began to itch.

On spring and summer afternoons we would go back to the white clapboard guest cottage, our kneecaps and ankles pricked by undergrowth, over felled trees, through a meadow of forget-me-nots in the humid, fragrant wood with our rabbits on the effigy poles and handfuls of the white, lacy flowers. We didn't bring the dogs because we weren't allowed to hunt with them. Only Vargas held that privilege. Vargas said we had to keep our hunting separate. He also told us that if we didn't eat meat our teeth would fall out and we would grow hair all over our bodies like werewolves (facts we verified in one of his medical journals). If we wanted to keep healthy we had to learn to trap and hunt. Fishing would have been ideal because there was a lake an hour's walk through the forest (according to our maps) but Vargas didn't like us eating fish, or venturing that far off alone. We studied hunting manuals and practised in the field until we were capable. The snares weren't that difficult and the yield was adequate.

In the autumn we were allowed to accompany Vargas on a number of deer hunts with the crossbow. The cleanest kill was the one that hit the heart. If done correctly the animal would drop dead in its tracks. Once, Vargas shot a charging stag in the chest. It died with its head down so that its enormous rack of antlers was staked fast into the ground. Vargas called his men in with a walkie-talkie and they came with a four-by-four to pull it out. We hid in the bushes until they were gone.

The first time we were brought out on the deer hunt marked yet another devastating event in our years under the Doctor's captivity. He told us we had to slit the throat and drink the blood. We both knew that there was no way out and obeyed, doing our best to perform the tasks dead-faced. The deer's blood was salty and rich and tasted no different from our own. The bodies were cut up and stored in a freezer in the basement. Vargas ate most of the kill but forced us to eat it as well as the rabbits, for health reasons. He taught us to make jerky in the smoke house. Then he took the heads and skins and gave us lessons in the art of taxidermy and tanning. We spent many hours perfecting his trophies and rugs. Out of the hooves and shins we made rattles which we kept at the cabin in the woods where we had crafted them according to an account in one of the books on Midwestern Native American tribes. The rattles were used as instruments to cure as well as to call bison. Camille and I were allowed all of the rabbit pelts and made jackets and boots out of them for our Barbie dolls.

Our mother's tragedy did nothing to dispel Dr Vargas's love of apiculture. He kept five hives. We ran through the swarming hum, picking up speed until we came to the white clapboard cottage and went round the back to the roasting pit where we stuck our rabbit poles into the earth and set about making a fire. In the winter we generally made stews. While the bodies were cooking on the spit we would experiment with teas and potions in the cottage, Pan's Elixir being among them.

In the first two years of captivity we were under Vargas's tutelage day and night. As it so happened, as well as being a psychiatrist and psychoanalyst, he was also a gymnastics instructor with qualifications from Romania. We practised in the barn which he had converted into an Olympic-standard gymnasium. Here, there, and everywhere this dark master imposed upon us a viciously circumscribed, authoritarian, dogmatic and anti-magical system – the mortal enemy of anyone committed to a magical universe in which all is spontaneous, unpredictable, and alive.

Vargas was a firm believer in modern science (whilst Camille and I, in secret, had disproved all of its basic tenets). Part of his science included classical conditioning. Before the study sessions he would begin with something like, "The tigers of wrath are wiser than the horses of instruction," the cue to fasten the electric dog collars around our necks. For every wrong answer we got a shock. Before discovering the collars he had used a pencil which left a triangle of lead dots on the back of my hand, resembling a Triad tattoo. Camille always flinched and ended up getting stabbed in the upper arm or the wrist which broke the pencil and failed to mark her. Dr Vargas sat opposite us with the two remote control boxes on the kitchen table, his fingers on the dial, antenna pointed toward us, his breath stinking of rotting milk, lips parted – lips we were forced to kiss each night at bedtime.

I don't recall exactly when Camille and I began to notice the acute lift in sensitivity to our environment. The effects were remarkably similar to accounts described in one of the anthropology books concerning a tribal people called the Desana of the Colombian Amazon. Camille referred to it as 'jungle sensitivity' after reading a similar account by the scholar Colin Wilson. In this state the spheres of our perception became amplified, the longitudes and latitudes of our sensibilities expanded. The flora, fauna, rocks, wind – in short, all of the forces of Nature – spoke to us. Camille developed the ability to smell water and locate underground reservoirs which we discovered whilst visiting friends and patients of Dr Vargas at the site of their new home near the Acadian mountains, scouting for a place to drill a well. Vargas became more of an open book. We were able to smell his agitation, his joy, his cruelty, like certain animals can. The scent of where he had spent the last twenty-four hours and vaguely what he had done hung on his clothing. We read him like a medium in a trance picking up visions, uninhibited by time and space.

The dogs were relegated to an old grain silo Vargas used as a kennel. There were bales and mountains of hay and heat lamps, as well as blankets the dogs slept on. Still, it was for the most part cold and damp in the winter and through until the end of spring. We were only allowed a couple of hours with them a day and would usually go for a walk in the woods and then sit with them, in the hay. I don't know who fed them at this point; we were no longer allowed. A constant concern was that Dr Vargas had also been experimenting on them. We saw traces of his work. The thought was too much to bear.

During the bi-weekly poker sessions (where Vargas would inevitably conjure tales of the Monte Carlo Casino's history and Beaux Arts magnificence where we would someday break the bank with our poker skills as Joseph Jagger had done at the roulette tables in 1873), we quenched our vengeance, baiting and confounding him, drawing out the tension and anxiety to the point of over-exertion, then finally driving the spike in hard and deep and crudely as we watched him squirm. He was not worthy of a clean kill. Needless to say, the Doctor's vanity was greatly piqued by our impossible winning streaks which so far had granted us a visit to one of the libraries we had not yet seen with five books for Camille and three for myself. Camille and I did our best to keep our abilities a secret, but we had more and more accidents. Our abnormal behaviour sent Dr Vargas into a depraved euphoria of experiments to test the newfound abilities.

Then, one day, just as the powers had appeared, so they vanished. Dr Vargas doubted and called us whores, then disappeared into the back woods for several days where we later discovered he had deepened the roasting pit so that a ladder or rope was necessary to climb out of it. There we spent roughly the next two weeks, unclothed, fed on deer jerky and water. I vaguely recall the night he appeared at the edge of the pit clothed only in his underwear and threw down a rope and we climbed up, gaining purchase with our feet in the packed earth until we reached the top. The Doctor was quivering and in a state of mental confusion, as though the idea had suddenly come to him in sleep and he was half awake – a grunting somnambulist.

We were matriculated in the first year of middle school under the names Jane and Susan Doe. Phase two in our education included a re-socialisation programme. We stopped hunting rabbits and became versed in the culinary arts. It was imperative we learn how to move like ghosts among the general population. We were to acquire the skills of espionage, infiltration, and sabotage most often attributed to ninjas. Betraying our General – Dr Vargas – would result in inconceivable tortures and horrors. We had seen evidence of what he was capable of, and it was clear

– depravity teemed in vicious hordes over every aspect of his soul.

Idle chit-chat was as an excellent shield against snooping interlocutors but even so, it was best kept to a minimum as it could lead to a slip of the tongue. Vargas warned us that the other children would no doubt make us suffer and said whatever didn't kill us would make us stronger.

Under Vargas's direction we slipped by easily unnoticed after an initial period of being pegged as snobs, held in contempt and shunned. From this vantage point we were able to carry out our missions. Occasionally schoolyard gossip would turn to Vargas. The general consensus held that he was a blood-sucking vampire and baby killer. It was true, Dr Vargas did, to some extent, have an air of Klaus Kinski in *Nosferatu* about him, except that his teeth fit properly in his mouth, his fingernails were shorter and he moved with more speed and agility. Vargas chose to cover his baldness from the world with a thick, black, luxuriant toupee he wore with authority. We had watched the film in French class and there had been talk of how Camille and I were the spitting images of Isabelle Adjani. The film imprinted within us a special kind of terror that evil would prevail, hanging over our slumbering bodies like incubi, terrorising our dreams.

By this time, in high school, the teachers and students began to notice us again. Boys stopped us in the hallways, pinned us into corners and dropped amorous notes in our lockers. We were taunted, threatened and kicked on a regular basis by a posse of the most popular girls – long-legged, cherubim-cheeked, sylph-like, French-kissing, tequila-drinking hell-raisers. They were all bisexual with two of them sharing the same boyfriend, Japhy, seventeen – a boy with the decisively masculine beauty of Laurent Marqueste's Perseus slaying Medusa and Kurt Cobain. One of these girls was the Vice Principal's daughter, Danielle. Dr Vargas invited her mother to tea and after an exchange of niceties, gave full disclosure of the situation. He was met with a studied, airheaded, Marilyn Monroe-like breathless incredulousness. "Danielle? Oh, Danni would never do that. No, not my Danni. We go to church every Sunday. Don't we, Danni? She sings in the choir." She smiled and brushed a curling tendril of hair from Danielle's cheek.

They didn't even make it to the cucumber sandwiches. Dr Vargas ordered them to leave. It was obvious he would have to take the matter straight to the top. This escalation – the exposure to our house and to Dr Vargas himself – was unprecedented. When they left we begged him to abandon the cause as it would only end in resentment and degradation. The whole charade – if one could call it that – had gone one step too far.

Arms akimbo in his powder blue Yves Saint Laurent suit with sweat patches under the arms, Dr Vargas resembled a deranged and whisky-crazed Las Vegas preacher waiting for the next shotgun wedding ceremony to begin. He laughed, and as his eyes became slits he told us (his posture suggested he was also telling a room full of people) in his idiosyncratic way of speaking, without any discernible regional accent, about how Danielle – a junior – was known as the biggest slut in the school and had spread her legs for the entire wrestling team, as well as for a few of the teachers. "I'll bet her mother doesn't know about *that*. She'd be *mortified*."

I remember, on this occasion, Camille had replied with one of her tamer displays of narrative disjunction, in that far-off voice of hers, "Altamira – that's where I would like to go – to the prehistoric caves where Miró became inspired. He made angel wings with hundreds of tiny eyes because if we look through the right eyes we can be saved. He starved himself until he hallucinated. That's how he made the dream paintings. I read it in the biography of Diego Rivera."

"Someday we'll go to Altamira, Camille. Just you and I," I whispered in her ear.

Dr Vargas rummaged through his pockets for pharmaceuticals. "Of course we'll go to Altamira. That's beside the point. All I want to do is protect you. You're being *threatened* for the love of God. It isn't right. What else can I do?" He swallowed several pills with a glass of champagne.

"Put us out of our misery." Camille delivered the lines deadpan as she mimed blowing her brains out with a handgun. Vargas pretended not to notice.

In our sixteenth year, Dr Vargas's mother passed away. We left Viktor and Shiloh for the first time in our lives and boarded a plane bound for Mexico. We were both solemn in the car, turned inward, sad we had to leave them and praying the separation would not kill them due to their emotional attachment to us. We had read that dogs could die, like people, of broken hearts. The plane ride was long and dull with a stopover in Dallas. Vargas assured us he would soon take us from this land of pagan psychodramas and Chevrolet to Paris, where he had lived and studied as a young man, obtaining a degree in psychiatry and psychotherapy. He picked up a pink-coated bar of popcorn at one of the airport shops with disdain and told us that it was symbolic of the kind of mental decay he had been lecturing us about.

The hot sun, fragrant jasmine and relentless blue sky of San Marcos reminded us of our former southern Californian home and the last time we had seen our mother alive, and also of Viktor and Shiloh. We heard her chiming voice around the bends of sunlit passages and felt her cool presence in the painful, shadowy rooms of the Vargas family home. On the day of the funeral we were left behind with the maids, bodyguards (Dr Vargas's brother was a public official – with a face like a film idol), gardeners, et cetera and so took the opportunity to explore. We asked one of the maids, Valentina, if she knew which room our mother had last occupied and were met with a look of incredulousness which melted into a warm, doe-eyed compassion when we turned our heads to the wall and began to cry as discreetly as possible.

She took us by the arms, spiriting us around the old hacienda, through drawing rooms, libraries, up a staircase, and outside along a veranda where an enormous Victorian brass gilded cage sat with two birds inside, their red foreheads fading to orange and yellow around the neck, wings with the colour of rust and iridescent blue. Valentina opened French doors to a light, airy room with high ceilings, pale walls, walnut furniture and a bed with white sheets embroidered with flowers.

"She slept here." On the dressing table was the fateful bottle of Fleurissimo, a silver comb and an ornate silver-plated Art Nouveau hairbrush adorned with cherubs and flowers. A couple of strands of her hair, the colour of Coca-Cola in the sun, were tangled in the boar bristles. I put the brush in my pocket. We looked in the drawers and in the closet for other signs of her but found nothing. Camille took the bottle of perfume.

"Come, niños." She waved her hand with a pained expression on her face. "Dr Vargas is back soon and would not be pleased to see you here." We followed Valentina out and stopped in front of the cage with the two birds inside. She leaned in toward us and whispered that they were Cuban Red Macaws, the last of their kind, and that their names were Osvaldo and Violetta. The birds were eating lice off one another, oblivious to our faces peering in through the gilded bars. We made clicking sounds and called their names. They stared at us sideways with quizzical looks.

Valentina raised a finger. "Very intelligent birds. Like children."

When Dr Vargas returned we were called to the library where we found him in a leather chair drinking bourbon. He motioned for us to sit down on a chintz sofa opposite in front of two fizzy lemonades. We listened to him as we stared into his crumpled face, searching it for any tells without giving away any of our own.

"We'll be going back in a matter of days, my darlings."
He flicked a piece of imaginary lint off of his sleeve.
"We're taking a couple of macaws with us. Summer in
that northern country is fleeting and – as I am sure you are
aware – tropical birds are at risk of expiring from draughts,
so we must take every precaution that they do not die.
They would be dead in an hour if I left them here with my
brother. We're going to drive back in a Winnebago." He
poured himself another drink and rolled his tongue over
his teeth. "When I'm gone this will all be yours. Yes, my
mother left everything to me. Not my good-for-nothing
brother. I'm letting him stay here, of course. We'll come
down a few times a year, no doubt. But ideally we shall be
installed in Paris, or the Côte d'Azur, within the next two
years, the time it takes to sell the house and re-establish
ourselves abroad. You've got to be educated properly. I
can't leave my legacy to cretins. Your mother had wanted
you to grow up in the wilds of Maine as she had done, but
honestly, I can't take much more of it." Camille sat erect
and shot lightning bolts out of her eyes at the man who did
not believe in magic. I took a sip of lemonade.

Our transcontinental voyage in the belly of the luxurious
beige-carpeted, dark-wooded interior of the Winnebago
spanned long weeks of ever-changing terrain through the
windows on either side as Dr Vargas drove furiously to
'The Three Bs' – Brahms, Bach, and Beethoven – popping
pills all the way, while Osvaldo and Violetta flew free,
defecating on practically every surface as sweating, flush-
faced Camille and I quickly erased every last goopy particle
with baby wipes. The air conditioning was *verboten*. Only

one window was to be opened a crack barely large enough for an ant to pass through. A net had to be set up separating the driving cockpit and the rest of the vehicle to keep the birds from dazing themselves on the expansive windshield in an attempt to fly out, as well as to keep them from ripping Vargas's other earlobe off. One of them (it was impossible to tell one from the other unless they spoke) had alighted on his shoulder during dinner one night and proceeded to tear his earlobe off with several quick jerks of the head. There was a lot of blood and Vargas ended up going to an Emergency Room, in some southern town I forget the name of, to get stitches.

It became clear that Osvaldo and Violetta saw Vargas as their mortal enemy. They would perch as close to the driver's seat as possible, hiss and repeat, "*Tito es el mal*", turn, lift their tails, and spurt faeces in his direction. He appeared oblivious.

After Mexico (and the road) the familiar mansion emerged out of the forest as if from another world. It felt strange to step onto solid land. The briny sea air mixed with the scent of sun-warmed forest was a delightful reprieve from the humid, stagnant insides of the Winnebago with its odour of Vargas's unwashed armpits. Three bees with elongated bodies flew out of the vehicle's door and disappeared into the pastoral woodland scene. Viktor and Shiloh had aged considerably. Great Danes do not live long, eight years maximum. We vowed we would never leave them again.

The birds were clever and thoughtful. We trained them to go in search of precious objects in Vargas's wing of the house which was forbidden to us. They came back with mother's rings and necklaces, hat pins, and gem-studded brooches, and once, two of her silk dresses. Osvaldo and Violetta continued with their secret vendetta against Vargas, ripping his expensive Italian shirts, dropping excrement on his head and giving him "love bites". He walked around with bandages on his ears and fingers, so enamoured with them that he only scolded lightly, in French.

The guest house was to be turned into a kind of atrium for the macaws with special "man trap" doors used in banks and in the diamond trade, to keep the cold air from infiltrating the tropical climate that was to be created to keep the birds alive. Work was to begin in a week so Camille and I had time to enjoy the last days of our cottage in the woods.

We were filled with terror and wonder (concealed behind artful poker faces) when Vargas came to the screen door of the cottage with a green-eyed, dark-haired girl (who looked to be our age), opened it, and introduced her as: "Betty." He and Betty's mother were having cocktails by the pool. Little did Betty and her mother know, they had walked straight into a trap from which escape would prove extremely difficult. Vargas's talk had lately turned to finding us a sibling and a mother. It was clear we had to act, and quickly. But how? All of our previous attempts had failed, even ones which had been well thought out. Camille and I remained calm and began to run through formulated plans.

It was one of those breezy days when the dewy scent of lilacs and humid forest fragrances spilled through the cottage, over our tea party scene – the three of us sitting primly at the table. Camille offered Betty a cup of Pan's Elixir. The girl thanked Camille, eyes fluttering across the table, hands toying with the edge of the doily within the closest proximity. I asked her how she had come to be here. She made like she was going to take a sip of the tea but then quickly explained that she and her mother had come to our region on vacation and met Dr Vargas at a restaurant in the village where he invited them to his chateau to meet his two daughters and go for a swim.

"Do you like croquet? We could always play croquet after our refreshment."

"Or badminton? Then perhaps go for a swim?"

Betty took a sip, set the tea cup down and wiped her mouth. "Yes. I'd like that very much."

Camille couldn't hold her tongue. "Betty, you and your mother are in danger. Dr Vargas kidnapped us and is holding us hostage. We have to find a way to get you and your mother out of here, or else you will suffer the same fate."

Betty began to choke, followed by convulsions and what appeared to be suffocation in front of our eyes – her pale hands, fluttering for a moment around her neck, then grasping for the table as her eyes rolled back in her head and she fell to the floor. Camille ran out for help, the screen door clacking behind her. I fell to the floor beside Betty and began CPR. I watched her face turn blue. She looked like a bruise on the carpet. Or Krishna. Or Shiva. Her mother was hysterical over her body. Vargas remained calm, picked her up and carried her to the Land Rover in the drive. Osvaldo and Violetta began to shriek, beating their wings frantically against the bars of their cage, poolside. One of them called out in a voice so like mother's it sent an iciness through me, coupled with a sinking feeling and finally a sickening of the heart: "God, *forgive me! I have cast us to the devil!*" We never saw Betty or her mother again.

The next day Vargas set fire to the largest patch of Pan's Elixir flowers in the wood. We got off lightly and were banished to our rooms after a belt whipping with raised arms in the shed. Vargas said he had done an autopsy on the body and it had been poison. He told us that the flowers used in the tea we gave Betty were poisonous. We were never to touch them again.

Camille's room was above mine so that we could talk to one another through the ventilation shafts. Our telepathy had returned but was unreliable and intermittent. Camille read from an encyclopaedia in her room: "*Conium maculatum.* A lethally poisonous herbaceous plant of the *Umb – umbelli-ferae* family related to parsley. The foliage is rank and finely divided. There are white, lacy flat-topped clusters of small flowers which erupt from a hollow, purple or red-mottled stem. Native to the Old World, the plant has been naturalized and is common in parts of the United States. The poisonous alkaloid coniine found in it causes paralysis, convulsions, and eventual death. The plant was used as a means of execution in ancient Greece and was the method used to kill the philosopher Socrates. It is considered an invasive plant in twelve U.S. states."

By my calculations, it did not seem to be outside the realm of possibilities that Camille and I were either dead, immune to the poison, or possibly even immortal. Before I could respond to Camille the nightly blast of noxious gas came through the shaft and I blacked out. When I awoke I found myself in bed, in a nightgown without any underpants on. A line from Whitman was scrawled across my left arm in black felt tip marker: *And your flesh shall be a great poem.* I undressed. All over my body was written: *Vargas.* All at once everything seemed artificial. Reality had become plastic, inorganic. I rubbed my arms in the bath with soap and a washcloth and it was as though I was rubbing a doll's arms. The ink would not wash off. The world appeared to be more abstract. I could not hold on to it. My hair also smelled like a Barbie doll's. That morning at the kennel we found Viktor and Shiloh cold and dead, stiff with rigor mortis, beside one another in the hay, their skeletal bodies curled up muzzle to muzzle. We knew they had escaped, that they were free, but still felt like an ancient Aztec sacrificial victims, our chests cut open with our still-beating hearts ripped out. We dug a hole for them both deep in the woods beside a boulder, said their last rites and wept every day thereafter beside their grave when we came to adorn their final resting place with prayers and flowers.

Weeks later, from the bedroom window of the guest cottage – peering through a set of binoculars – Camille and I noticed how the bees appeared to move in decidedly more aggressive than usual phalanxes around the apiaries. In fact, there appeared to be a war going on with three of the hives against the other two. A few days later we found a neighbourhood cat not far from them, bloated and lifeless. I told Camille how I had seen three bees – possibly of the Mexican killer variety – exit the Winnebago the day we came back. It was clear. We had to saturate Vargas's clothes with mother's Fleurissimo.

After the dowsing of Vargas's closet and bed sheets Camille and I bathed and went to bed. We awoke to Vargas's screams emanating from the back of the house. We watched him from the window, poolside, *sans toupee* in his tight European swim trunks flailing the red, Fleurissimo-saturated terrycloth robe around him in a frantic flamenco, repelling and attracting the bees which at one moment took on the shape of a bull that felled him to the tiles where he ceased to move.

I turned, expecting to see Camille's pale shoulder and wide eyes to share in the shock and wonderment, but she was gone. Perhaps three or four days passed. I searched the entire house and felt the phantoms of Viktor and Shiloh by my side as I called for Camille. Vargas's body disappeared. I went to the cabin every day, but Camille was never there. I left a note. I was suddenly struck with the thought that perhaps the rituals, potions, and practices we had been following had taken a turn. Had she managed the sophisticated manoeuvre of displacing herself in space and time? Yes, I believed, it was certainly possible Camille had disappeared and taken all physical evidence of her existence with her only to resurface in another location. A mere thought could have sent her to the first place that flickered in her mind at that instant. Blood rang in my ears.

I decided then and there that I would go to Altamira. I wondered about the man in our visions – the one we called Deadeye. When would he come? Was he near? I had to find Camille.

December 24th, Passamaquoddy Bay environs, Maine

Maynard found the small, navy backpack next to a birch, sunk into the snow. It must have been thrown from a distance because there weren't any tracks leading up to it. He picked the bag up then slowly turned, three hundred and sixty degrees. He would see what was inside when he got back to the cabin, but from the size and shape it felt like notebooks, maybe something else in the pockets, maybe something valuable. Once, when he was a teenager and lived in Boston, he'd found a diamond Cartier watch in a dumpster. That was the year before he enlisted. Now he did occasional jobs that paid good money and the rest of the time stayed away from people as much as possible.

Maynard took out a set of binoculars and aimed them for the reverse trajectory he suspected the bag had taken, adjusted the independent focus, and scanned the area. He stopped where there were tracks and blood and the evidence of a body dragged backward, leaving a mark like a snow angel killed on impact and hauled away. Then more footprints.

He called for his dog, Brigitte. The Bauceron came bounding through the heavy snow with a rabbit in her mouth and blood on her muzzle. Better not to get involved. He knew his neighbour was a doctor but had never seen the man up close. They stayed out of each other's business. Dr Vargas was the ideal neighbour as far as that went. Maynard had a police scanner at the cabin and could listen to see if anything was happening at the Vargas estate.

Maynard trudged back to the cabin in the violet light. His breath steamed the inside of the ski mask and irritated him – he put it out of his mind. Brigitte looked ecstatic with the rabbit hanging like a rag doll from her mouth, bounding through the birch and pine trees encrusted with ice, eventually disappearing from sight. Maynard wished he could be as happy as that dog. She was an excellent tracker. Keenly intelligent. She killed clean and well and efficiently and was more loyal than any man or dog he had ever known. He trusted her with his life. She was all he had in the world. He'd bought her in France as a pup from a breeder three years ago on a business trip.

The cabin in the woods was a picture postcard in the snow. Brigitte sat at the door, panting, with the rabbit laid out on the front step. They had been roaming through the woods for nearly five hours; Maynard had been unable to sleep. The night had been clear and they had been able to see the stars. He went to the side of the house and pissed in the snow, watching the steam rise, and felt almost as happy as he imagined Brigitte to be but it quickly passed. He then walked to the front door, picked up the rabbit, let the dog in and set the backpack down on the floor before going out to skin the rabbit by the shed. He'd been skinning rabbits for a while and he'd become good at it.

Inside the house was warm with the woodstove still going, if only dimly. He would have to add logs, possibly start a new fire. Maynard pulled the ski mask from his head, stepped on the heels of his boots and kicked them off. The rabbit was damp and limp, shining pink. He cut it up and fed it to Brigitte, piece by piece. He then cleaned the area, automatically, his thoughts already on the woodstove and the coffee he would make. After, he would see what was in the backpack.

When the coffee was made he stood with a cup by the woodstove, took a sip, then set it down and went to fetch the backpack, curiosity getting the better of him. He took it to an armchair not far from by the fireplace and sat down. Five thousand dollars in cash were strewn about in billfolds with rubber bands around them in between notebooks. In the front pocket were a few hairpins and a collection of small rocks, with what looked like a crystal among them. The seven notebooks were all numbered. There was also a legal notepad. The handwriting was frantic, in blue ink and had words and phrases crossed out among the paragraphs. The pages were meticulously numbered. He found the first entry and began to read.

May 1st – 5th, Interstate 15, Nevada

We are living in dark times, what Buddhists call the degenerate Third Age. The Jains believe our time is so toxic that no Buddha will be born to light the way. In order to attain lasting peace, harmony, the grace of the Almighty, and perhaps even our own survival as a human race, we must ignite the heavenly blaze on our own (a formidable undertaking). The only advantage being that in these hours of darkness our good deeds and thoughts are rewarded a thousandfold. William Blake had a modus operandi for perceiving the truth he called the "corrosive method" – a process which was a philosophy, as well as a method of embossing images and print onto metal. The idea was to incite revelation and uncover hidden aspects by "melting apparent surfaces away, and displaying the infinite which was hid."

Benoît Del Mar, a.k.a. Venus Acid Boy (a name he gave himself after misinterpreting Bjork's lyrics when she sang: "Venus as a boy...") had corroded me – he had seen deep inside and said "I do", kissing me like a cocaine-soaked cowboy, just as the tune on the radio turned over into full orchestration (he had a sixth sense for that). We became husband and wife at midnight under the stars, in our celadon, 1971 Cadillac Eldorado convertible, on the first day of May in a drive-thru wedding at the Chapel of the Bells just outside Las Vegas. After the ceremony, we drove through the desert under galaxies stretched like plasma across the sky, making vows to take the infamous city for as much as our luck, talent, and determination would allow. Ben drove. We rode the waves of adrenaline. There was a storm inside of us – a burning, howling thing.

We hit the 'Strip' (lit up like a pinball machine), then played roulette and no-limit Texas Hold'em at several establishments for three consecutive days and nights, turning two grand into sixty-three. It was a beautifully orchestrated smash and grab until the last casino where, four hours deep into our second game, we were apprehended by two smooth-skinned men resembling gigantic roly-poly toys in suits with special casino Sheriff badges pinned to them. Ben got a look like he was about to throw whisky in both of their faces and set them on fire, but thought the better of it. They escorted us out of the gaming area and walked us down a corridor where we were deposited in an empty lounge.

The two men stepped in, closed the doors behind them and conversed. It seemed they didn't know whether to hire us – or take us out into the desert and show us why we should never step foot in the state of Nevada again. One of the men noticed his gun was gone.

Benoît can turn on a hair trigger. One-thirteenth of a second is the time it takes for the most switched-on person's brain to receive information and for them to react to it. He was right up against that barrier – aiming for Bruce Lee's edge. They say Lee could move so fast the film had to be played back in slow motion to catch him striking his opponent. Ben produced the missing firearm seemingly out of thin air and squared himself with one of them – muzzle stuck to the man's forehead – before anyone could say 'spit'. His underhanded gaze was aimed at roly-poly number two who surrendered his weapon with a look of abject dread. Benoît stood there, effulgent, a gun in each hand, haloed in a bright leer of madness, blazing with pure killing purpose. He then explained how they were to proceed. The roly-polys did everything he said, to the letter. We played it nice and easy and walked out with one of them, leaving the other unconscious and handcuffed to a floor-mounted bar stool. The three of us stopped at the cage, picked up our winnings with the roly-poly's corroboration, then exited the building.

We dumped the goon in the middle of nowhere with a bottle of water after about thirty miles. On the way, he told us we better get used to being ghosts because we'd just signed our lives away to the devil, we didn't know who we were dealing with, that from the moment we saw the back of his head the hounds of hell would be on our trail, et cetera, et cetera.

The plan was to keep moving, straight ahead. Dust, pollen and insects flashed in the headlight beams. Agile and calm, face lit up in the dash lights, Benoît changed gears. His blonde hair was close-cropped, a military cut. He had a beautiful curve to the back of his head. The cassette player played a tune with distorted synth pads through a melody with harps and strings and ominous church bells, driven by a fat analogue kick and a funeral march snare roll. Ben eased down on the accelerator, head nodding to the beat, hand light on the wheel.

I put my arm out the window into the air currents. The desert sky spanned out deep violet against the inky lines of Joshua trees, tentacled and bushy, armies of them, flanking the highway. Rock formations turned past from all angles. The horizon line glowed phosphate green, then bled into a thin band of sangria.

I leaned against Benoît, stared out the windshield and played the incident in the casino over in my mind. I had never seen him with a gun but knew he had spent two years in the army. He certainly appeared to be familiar with firearms. This wasn't the first time I had seen him act in a violent manner, but every time there was good reason. Once he kicked a man senseless, breaking his own foot in the process. There were times I thought he was a magnet for conflict, even though he never brought anything on directly. It was always in defence of someone else. He was just that kind of man. I knew he would protect me at all costs.

We crossed state lines and into California, got rid of the guns, stopped at a pharmacy for hair dye and other essentials, then pulled up to a drive-thru hamburger joint and had hamburgers, milkshakes and fries. We took to the highway again and stopped at the third roadside motel we saw, the Dew Drop Inn.

When I stepped out of the car and looked around me I realised the last time I'd stood on southern Californian soil Camille was by my side and the attack of killer bees that ended our mother's life had not yet transpired. We must have been nearly ten. Who would have guessed that all of this tragedy would befall us, that we would lose one another and that I would journey so far and wide and come to this spot, newly married, running from casino mafia and the law?

The night had become a bright, well-bleached morning. Inside the room was decent and clean enough. It looked like it hadn't been redecorated since the Fifties – fake wood-panelled walls depicted deer hunting scenes, a white linen spread-covered bed in the centre, dark furniture backed up against the walls. The windows were open and it smelled like summer with the breeze coming through. We listened to the portable cassette player, took a shower together, smoked cigarettes then made love and waited for the adrenaline to clear out of our bloodstreams. I ran the tips of my fingers over Benoît's back until he stopped twitching and fell asleep.

I'd set what few of the childhood photographs I possessed on the night table after I'd opened my suitcase. The first shot could have been me or Camille, in a blur of Californian sun, aged three (the year my father left my mother for his Danish lover), standing in our grandmother's back garden on the neatly cut grass, gazing into space in a white flowered frock and white shoes. Camille's thin legs. Her sun-bleached, russet-brown, bobbed hair. Her pale skin. Long lashes. Her plump cheeks and little chin tilted slightly downward – perhaps ensorcelled by an insect? She, or I, was half in the mottled shadows and half in the sun.

The bush of rhododendrons behind her head made a violet crown of flowers with bright pink pistons. That may have been the last time we saw our father. No, I remember when we were six and he drove us to the gates of some place where we were given blankets and taken underground with other children.

It was still light outside and the bedside dial clock read nearly seven. Ben lay sprawled out on the bed, his head turned toward me. There was no place I would rather be but beside him. Even though we were possibly being hunted down by the Las Vegas mafia as well as the police. Our odds of getting out unscathed seemed to be around twenty percent. Ben had some experience with Mafioso types in France but, in the end, we had no familiarity with any of their M.O.s, outside the cinema. All that was left to us was an animal instinct and logic.

One thing was evident, we had to ditch the car and lay low. If we were feeling especially keen we could always wear disguises, hit one last casino, deposit the winnings in an American bank account, then step immediately on a plane for somewhere in Europe, Luxembourg perhaps, drain the account and disappear. But even that sounded like madness. We had to lay low. I made plans to bleach and dye my hair. We had to prepare to leave the country immediately, even if that meant driving to Mexico.

Ben had awoken and was taking drags off a cigarette as we sat there, pressed to one another, his arm around me, smoke spiralling upward and across the room with a ghost-like, ethereal quality to it, reminding me of the Bön deities Camille and I used to conjure up to guide and protect us.

The more often we addressed them, the greater the bond and the greater the knowledge that came to us. Camille had said, time and time again, "If you do not acknowledge their existence by contacting them, nor do everything in your power to gain their favour, they will leave you by the wayside to fend for yourself." I imagined their sylph-like forms, sitting by the bedside, guarding the doors and windows, standing watch over the motel grounds, traversing the sky above us. I asked them to protect us.

On the sheets were tiny rust explosions of dried blood. My knees were raw from riding Benoît in the night.

"You are sweet as peaches, baby." Ben put his hand on my naked ass and gave it a firm squeeze as we stared into one another's eyes and I watched as his began to burn.

"Like the Chinese peaches of Immortality?"

"Baby, you terrorize me." He killed his cigarette in the ashtray. "I'm going to have to start calling you the Terror." He pulled me close and I slid on top of him where I began to kiss his chest all the way down and couldn't help thinking it might taste of snow, and found that it did, like bright, Alpine snow, so cold that it burned and then tasted of iron as a feverish heat spread through me.

[FADE TO BLACK]

Dazed, lying in the cool dusk breeze, our bodies hot as stars, I thought of the moment we first met, under the pines, at a clifftop party in southwestern France – Benoît bare-chested with a horned helmet in his hand, illuminated in the labyrinth of forest shadows and sunlight. I had wandered down a path that led away from the revellers, heard a voice behind me and turned.

It was clear that he and I were made of the same volatile substance. A part of me shot out to him while the physical body remained rooted to the spot. I heard myself say, "*Salut.*" He smiled so that I saw the dimples in his cheeks and he seemed about to say something when I bounded off in the opposite direction. I didn't know what else to do in that moment. The heat was too much. I thought I might explode and disintegrate.

The second meeting followed soon after, on my birthday, the first of June. Again it was an impromptu, illegal gathering in the wilds of the Var, the location accessible only to those with the hotline number that changed periodically. This time the rave was in the back country, in a small valley.

It had been hell getting there in the tiny Fiat crammed with my boyfriend and his friends, praying the undercarriage would hold together, that the axle wouldn't break, navigating backroads, looking out for rocks. Our arrival without incident seemed a miracle. The scene looked something out of the film *Mad Max* but instead set in the verdant wilds of southern France. Tents and trucks with a few metal sculptures, as well as numerous captured municipal and roadwork signs and lights scattered here and there made up the village. There were several bonfires and a pig roasting on a spit.

With their gauged earlobes, tattoos, nose rings and other piercings, dreadlocks and shaved patches of hair they made for a wild bunch and maybe even a bit like Ötzi the Iceman's people who had lived nearby in what is now

Italy, five thousand years ago. The sound system sat in the approximate centre of the campsite where a wall of speakers stacked on top of one another ran perhaps thirty feet along, broken in the centre by a DJ booth not unlike a hunting blind which a hundred or so people danced in front of. The world outside might as well have collapsed. Dogs ran this way and that. Other members of the party were scattered between converted trucks or else in couples or groups in the grass under the sky that blazed blue overhead. The general feeling was that it could continue on for days. We were in the middle of nowhere, behind cliffs which acted as a rampart higher than any man had ever built. No one would hear us.

The sun was shining; it was about four in the afternoon. Drugs appeared in abundance as we walked through the crowd. My boyfriend, if he was still my boyfriend, kissed me on the cheek and said he was going with his friends and would see me around. I could tell in the way he spoke to me and in his body language that it was over. Our relationship had come to an end. I watched him walk away through a blur of tears.

In retrospect, it was a mistake to stay at his parents' house after he'd left and moved in with a girl from his university for two weeks. For whatever reason, he'd come back only recently. His parents were disenchanted with me and I knew I deserved their disdain. I should have found new lodgings immediately, asked an acquaintance in the next village over if I could stay with him for a week to get my head straight and perhaps go to Monaco rather than stay with the family and hope that my boyfriend would come back for me. I was unravelling. More than anything in that moment I wanted a spliff, and congratulated myself on the foresight to have pre-rolled ten of them. I even had a lighter. I lit up and walked toward the sound. I would have to find a ride back as soon as possible, even if that meant walking to a main road and hitch-hiking. But as I was there, and it was my birthday, I could stay until tomorrow afternoon and then find a lift back.

Growing ever closer to the wall of speakers, I gave in to the narcotic pull of the music. The bass pressed on my chest and gave me the sensation of being lifted off the ground, while other frequencies played on my synapses, lulling me into reveries of ecstatic euphonies. Was this what the prehistoric people who gathered in a subterranean hypogeum on the island of Malta had experienced when they held rituals to their gods? The underground structure had been purpose built to transform and augment sound so that altered states could be reached – the very walls vibrated with their chants and instruments. It must have appeared as though divine music poured from the stone.

In the centre of this hypogeum, known to archaeologists as the Hypogeum of Hal-Saflieni, is a chamber referred to as The Oracle Room. When low notes within the male vocal range are sung, or in the case of certain prehistoric drums, the modulations can be heard throughout the structure magnified a hundredfold, causing the walls to vibrate. Scientists found that these sound waves altered human brain patterns and induced hypnagogic states as they fired the creative centres of the brain. The longer I remained drugged in the music, the closer I felt to Camille. We had danced like this, shaking rattles, with one of us on the drum – in homage to the various pagan deities and nature spirits we happened to be calling the attentions of. Camille's eyes had shone with visions of other worlds she assured me were all around us. Most people remained blind to them because one had to learn to 'see' with another kind of vision that could only be attained through the proper exercises and teachings. These hidden universes held knowledge we sought for our transformation into warriors. A supreme vigilance had to be maintained until it was a habit, until we became impeccable. Like this, the signs could be observed, we had only to interpret them correctly.

It was possible Camille had been trapped in one of these "invisible" places. In which case, despite the perils, I was going to have to do everything I could to resuscitate her teachings and carry them out to perfection. I remembered her performing ancient Greek rites among the oak trees where we came into contact with supernatural beings, drawn to our Dionysian frenzy like moths to a flame. We were transported to their world for what seemed like both an eternity and an instant.

The rave created an atmosphere which had similarities with our interpretations of the ancient rites, and was perhaps also capable of luring otherworldly life forms to its spectacle. It was worth a try. I danced and emptied my mind of thought, the crucial first step to going beyond 'everyday' reality. Once the internal dialogue ceases, another way of perceiving is revealed, so that one can enter into the other worlds. I recalled other fragments of Camille's teaching and acted upon them.

For the most part the crowd danced steadily in their body paint, goggles, masks and helmets, some with antlers, facing the humming wall of sound like an army intent on liberation. A few fell from the ketamine but after ten minutes or so were up and moving again as though nothing had happened, which unfortunately was one of the consequences of using the drug in such high doses. No doubt their revival was often precipitated and fortified by the abundant, circulating cocaine. Dogs ran back and forth and in circles and sometimes nearby, but most remained at a distance, running amongst other canines and clusters of people dotted about the landscape.

The torch had been passed to the French by a small group of young men and women from southern England who called themselves The Heretix and began what was to become a 'Free Party' movement that spread across Europe. They had organized gatherings, 'free parties', or raves, that traversed the British Isles until their activities were declared illegal by the Crown, forcing them to flee across the Channel where they moved from place to place in a small convoy beginning in France, outrunning the law, making parties, spreading the gospel with their acid house and techno. Later they left and made their way across the continent to India. France, where citizens burn cars to express their civil disobedience, was fertile soil for the movement. It spread like wildfire across the country with hundreds of small tribes forming.

The 'free parties' were acts of civil disobedience as much as they were hedonistic expressions devoted to the music and experiments in alternative living which was perhaps closest in spirit to a collectivist form of anarchism. They lived in tribes, worked and bought food and gas for their vehicles when they could; otherwise they siphoned big rigs and stole from grocery stores. Selling drugs allowed for pricier objects like sound system equipment.

As the gatherings grew to thousands they were called 'Teknivals' and took place in fields with perhaps a hundred or more sound systems participating, police helicopters flying overhead. Equipment was seized, unarmed party-goers were beaten with clubs, arrests were made. The people did not give up however, they continued on. Then the riot police were called in. A civilian's hands were blown off when a grenade was launched into the crowd; no doubt under the influence of a combination of mind-altering drugs, he simply caught whatever it was he saw flying through the air, not suspecting it would be an explosive. Exposure of the 'free party' phenomenon grew in the media. A documentary film was made and shown on a national television channel where undercover night cameras were used to capture the dizzying hordes in various states of agony and ecstasy with drug dealers among them calling out their wares. Psychologists interviewed for the film concluded that it was not altogether unhealthy – the youth forming social groups which in many ways emulated the tribal societies of our ancestors was not in itself a threat to their mental health. The dancing and crying out was, in fact, a particularly effective means of relieving built-up inner tensions. The MDMA in itself (assuming it was pure) was not necessarily harmful if taken infrequently, perhaps a few times a year in reasonable doses, but they drew the line at the rest of the drugs – ketamine, cocaine, nitrous oxide, cannabis, and LSD. Anyone who used these substances needed immediate medical and psychiatric attention.

It felt as though I had been dancing for a very long time but the sun had hardly moved in the sky. I wandered away from the dancefloor and made my way along a string of parked cars, stopping to admire the view and light a spliff. I would have to find water. I heard someone call out, a male voice, and I turned around. It was the boy with the horned helmet from the other party on the cliff side, motioning to me to approach him where he sat in the back seat of an otherwise empty old, black sedan. I approached and stood in the full sunlight above him, looking down at his boyish, handsome face, his dark eyes with dilated pupils. He spoke in an easy manner, "You remember me?"

"Yes, of course." We spoke in French. He offered me a cigarette. I asked him if he had anything to drink; he handed me a can of Coca-Cola. I offered him the joint. He took it and said he'd roll another one for me, that there was some hashish in the glove compartment, then reached over the front seats, pressed a cassette into the cassette player, got the smoking materials and sat back, motioning for me to sit beside him. I climbed into the back seat. "I don't think we've been properly introduced, I'm Benoît."

"Enchanted. I'm Eugenie."

"You're not French. Your accent is American or Scandinavian."

"American."

"From where?"

"All over, but I was born in California."

"I'd love to go to the States one day," he said and grinned.

We sat, smoked, and listened to the music. The sound was acid house, but more progressive with techno, jazz and even dub beats. There were samples from orchestras, Edith Piaf, Nina Simone. It struck me at points that the mix was as glorious and fiendishly complex as one of Bach's fugues – lines and phrases engaged in a hunt, echoing one another, existing independently yet also harmoniously. Benoît said it was a recording of something he'd recently made on his machines. I told him I thought it was a work of genius, that he was ahead of his time.

He stole slow and even glances at me as he leaned on the window frame, smoking the spliff, his movements relaxed and easy, then asked me about where I'd come from, what I was doing here, what my dreams and hopes and plans for the future were. We listened to another mix and smoked more hashish. He told me he'd grown up in foster homes and was finally adopted by a fifty-year-old woman who had already raised a son who became a lawyer. She was kind and loving, smoked cannabis and went to raves in abandoned hangers, forests and fields. In the summer she went on the festival circuit. Her main source of income was selling knick-knacks from India and hashish. He'd broken her heart the day he joined the armed forces and was sent abroad. In the end, it was one of the biggest mistakes of his life. Not something he wanted to speak of. "Come with me, let's get out of here. Let's go for a ride down the coast." He launched himself over the front seats and turned around to me with the key in his hand. "Are you coming?"

I felt safe with him and didn't want to part company with him. I shut the door and climbed into the front. We drove on roads that snaked downward through the mountainous landscape until we came to the Mediterranean and continued along the coast to Cannes. Once there we turned back up into the foothills. It was not far from where Benoît said a gypsy friend of his had taken up with a girl who lived on her grandmother's estate. They had been staying with her for a month. She was, perhaps, a tobacco heiress.

"Si vous n'aimez pas la mer... si vous n'aimez pas la montagne... si vous n'aimez pas la ville... allez vous faire foutre!" Benoît did an impression of Belmondo from *À bout de souffle,* a film which had made an enormous impression on Camille and me as teenagers and placed the director Godard within our firmament of heroes. There had been a time when we had lived and breathed the New Wave, changed by its implications, invigorated by its vision, and made films with a handheld Bolex 8mm camera, found by one of Camille's familiars, a squirrel, in the attic. I couldn't see this squirrel and told her so. She said that Plato had had a familiar too and everyone thought he was mad, but the proof was in the tangible evidence the supernatural being provided. We also wrote letters to Godard, which were never sent because we were forbidden stamps. He had even persuaded some of the teachers at school to look out and inform him if they saw us with any, as well as a list of other contraband, such as chewing gum, sugary snacks, and fizzy drinks. Dr V always found us out. He said it was futile to try and pull the wool over his eyes because he had x-ray vision and could see through anything.

Ben leaned over the steering wheel, turned to me and smiled mischievously, reaching for his cigarettes. He offered me one, then tapped the base of the pack on the wheel, sending one flying into the air, which he caught in his mouth with an upward tilt of the head. I lit his cigarette. We meandered up dirt roads through the hills until we came to the gates of the house. Benoît's dog came bounding up to the car as we approached. She was large with a lanky gait and sizable floppy ears – clearly still in her puppyhood. "That's Gisele."

"She's beautiful." It was the same breed of dog that had accompanied the man we called Deadeye, from our childhood visions in the Maine woods. I wondered whether it was a sign or simply coincidence. Ben later told me she was a special guard and shepherding breed, difficult to obtain outside of France. Perhaps Deadeye was French.

Benoît's converted truck stood at the edge of the gravel drive, in all its glory. It was a Mercedes from the Sixties, painted merlot, all rounded edges and chubby curves and ovoid headlights. What appeared to be a Fifties model ambulance was soldered onto the top of the truck's cabin to make a kind of cockpit. Riveted behind this cockpit was the stern of a metal sailboat with a rounded back and porthole windows so that the deck made a terrace on top. The curves of Mercedes had been respected and it had been riveted and soldered together by the hand of an expert, as far as I could see.

Benoît and Gisele had a happy reunion and ended up on the grass, rolling over one another, wrestling and playing chase across the lawn that bordered the drive.

The heiress was very hospitable, very blonde, with an oval, delicate face like angels in medieval paintings. Her name was Clara. She was mad about Benoît's friend, Tristan, but played it very cool and never gave the game away, not to him at least. French women have a knack for being aloof and inaccessible to the point that it creates a great desire in the object of their affection. Clara didn't need to tell me in words how much she had been taken by her lover. And, when all was said and done, Tristan was like Ben, the kind of man that could easily make a woman go mad.

Benoît had been given a suite on the second floor with a view of the granite Neo-Gothic chateau through the pines (grandmother's house), and a swimming pool tiled like an oriental tapestry below.

"I'll take you back to the party or anywhere you want to go, at any time." He stood in front of his mixer and studio equipment arranged on a table against the wall and proceeded to flick switches and turn knobs so that music came out of the monitor speakers. "What do you want to drink? We have pretty much everything here."

"Rum?"

"On the rocks? Neat?" He searched through the liquor cabinet.

A warm tom-tom drum beat had begun the track with rattles and bongos coming in, layered over low, reverent, rolling basslines. Percussive sounds erupted out of nowhere, bright like fireworks against an otherworldly, ever changing landscape of synth melodies. More sounds appeared – the tossing of coins and a passage with a light, xylophone melody – accelerating and taking off with a drop followed by a quivering flock of stringed instruments over the churning, driving basslines.

Ben poured two glasses and handed me one, raising his to mine. "You have to look me in the eyes, when we say '*santé*', or else it's bad luck."

We looked one another dead straight and drank. Ben lit the joint that had been behind his ear and took a couple of tokes to get it going before passing it to me. The rum was very smooth with a hint of spice with caramel overtones.

"Diplomatico, it's the best."

I put my drink down on the nearest coaster. That afternoon I'd hopped out of a cramped car into a forest rave with my boyfriend who had then abandoned me. I no longer had a home. Now I stood in a room with a near stranger who looked like a film star from the Sixties and exuded a mesmeric hold over me, which ordinarily would have been unsettling but in this case felt safer than I had ever known.

"Something about you, Eugenie. I can tell you're going to make my life much more difficult."

"How so?"

"In the near future I know I'm going to be called away and it won't be easy leaving you."

"Are you going into the army?"

"No," he smiled. "They wouldn't have any more of me, nor I of them."

"I have to be home, near Nice, in about twenty-four hours anyway."

"Anytime, anywhere you want to go, just say the word. I'm at your service." He drank his rum in one go. "Sometime you'll have to hear me play at a party."

"Yes." I got very close to him. He took my hand and set his drink down and led me into the bedroom, closing the door behind us. The rest happened very slowly and tenderly at first but soon became heated. At one point my necklace burst, the tiny crystal beads scattering all over us and the bed, falling to the ground, hitting the carpet, shivering and rolling across the wooden floor.

I had been wearing the necklace for over a month to increase my odds of communication with Camille. Crystals are capable of conducting and storing information which can then be extracted, as is the case with light. If used properly they facilitate and amplify communications and perception, with a range that could possibly reach the other dimensions the quantum physicists and mystics speak of.

Had Camille sent me a message? If so, I had no clue as to what it meant. Later I gathered up as many of the crystals as I could and put them into a matchbox.

Our lovemaking lasted three days. We slept well and ate well and took a long walk with Gisele every afternoon in the hills. Each morning fresh pastries and coffee appeared in the kitchen, to be replaced by lunch and then dinner in the evening. There were plenty of leftovers for Ben's dog.

We crossed paths with Tristan and the heiress only once, skinny-dipping at night in the pool. Like the majority of the 'free party' people, Ben and Tristan spoke Verlan in the long standing French tradition of transposing syllables of individual words to create new ones with the same meanings. 'Verlan' itself came from the word 'l'envers', or inverse, which could be further 'verlanized' to 'lan-ver'. Woman – 'femme' – for example, becomes 'meuf' because the '*e*' in '*femme*' is silent. '*Meuf*' can also be 'verlanized' further to create '*feumeu*'. Cop, or '*flic*' becomes '*keuf*'. Words with more syllables like '*cigarettte*' have greater possibilities and can yield '*garetsi*' or '*retsiga*'. My ex-boyfriend had made use of Verlan but not to the point Benoît and Tristan expressed themselves in the language. Even Clara said she could barely understand what they were saying when they spoke that way. Still, I paid attention and absorbed as much as I could.

The next day Benoît and Tristan got word they were needed in Paris. I suspected I should have been back in Nice the previous day. My phone had run out of battery and if my ex-boyfriend had returned home before me they would worry and I would have, yet again, caused more strife for the family. We got in the car and left Gisele behind with Tristan and Clara to wait for Benoît's return from bringing me back. Afterwards they would take Benoît's truck north to Paris and meet their comrades.

We drove eastward along the coast, the reverse of the way we had come, in the bright sunshine with diamonds of light flashing off the Mediterranean, coasting along past the magnificent ochre, orange and red hued cliff sides of the French Riviera with the Alps snow-capped and shining in the distance, rising toward the impossibly blue sky like great cathedrals. They would remain long after I was gone. I had to focus on my immortality. Camille had taught me that this posture burned off the fear that kept us from perceiving the splendour and wonder of it all. Without the awareness of death everything is ordinary and trivial. As death stalks each and every one of us it presses upon us the magnitude of the mystery of life. This was what I had to remember.

The adventure with Benoît had certainly done something to me. I couldn't place any hope in our union continuing, however. He seemed serious, like he meant to come back, yet the chances of it actually happening appeared remote given the circumstances. Neither of us spoke at the beginning of the journey. Ben smoked cigarettes and stared ahead.

After a while I asked him to tell me more about what he had been doing, before he met me. Benoît explained that several years previously, after being decommissioned from the army, he had returned to Lyon. There he fell back in with guys from his *lycée* who had become involved in the Free Party movement, the same sorts of parties his adoptive mother had gone to. Eventually he went to her and they were reconciled. He took a job in construction, saved up and bought turntables and records. Then came the machines, an Akai MPC60, and others for filters, delays, reverbs, distortions, et cetera. He began to DJ at small parties in the woods outside Lyon, then in the summer he and his friends decided they would do a season of Teknivals. He bought a truck, fixed it up with the help of his friends and they were off with a mobile home and music studio.

They'd travelled across France, Italy and Spain attending Teknivals and small forest raves, marauding, siphoning gas, stealing from supermarkets, taking handouts from the clergy as well as dealing in large quantities of hashish, MDMA, and occasionally when they were desperate, cocaine. It had been a crazy ride. They'd gotten into trouble. The worst was quite possibly in Spain where he, Tristan, another Breton and a guy from Toulouse were passed in a square by skinheads who proceeded to run alongside the sidewalk traffic spraying everyone with OC aerosol, including children, which spurred Ben and his friends to action, grabbing the nearest weapons they could find which included a metal pipe and a ham shank in hot pursuit. Eventually the Policía Nacional ran Benoît down, beat him to the ground and hit him repeatedly on the head so violently they left him deaf in his right ear with a metal plate in his skull and a scar on his face.

We came around the edge of Nice and the crescent-shaped coastline, continuing northeast toward the mountains where I lived in one of the medieval hilltop villages that formed a chain of thirteen along the *Route des Villages Perchés* – a route that featured in Alfred Hitchcock's 1955 romantic thriller with Grace Kelly and Cary Grant as a jewel thief. We said goodbye on the corniche that wound around the foothills not far from the house. He told me the only thing that could stop him was death and that when he returned he would park in the village square and wait until I came. We decided to meet there rather than rely on mobile phones as they had a tendency to get lost and sit for days out of battery in Ben's world. If I decided to go to anywhere, Monaco for instance, I was to leave a note in the local post office for him. He would find me no matter what. He made me promise to take care of myself. We kissed again through the open driver's window and I turned to take a path through the forest that led toward my destination. I made my way down the familiar path and felt as though I had a double and was watching myself from some secret place. Was all of this happening? Was I truly leaving? Yes, of course, I had to and it was long overdue.

Thankfully, no one was home. I packed my things quickly, left quietly and placed an envelope with money and a note on the kitchen table. Once outside, I took a trail that wound under pine, cedar, and chestnut trees, then through olive and fig orchards that led to a meadow where a stone cottage fallen to ruin sat on the other side, near the ford that ran down the foothills. I continued on along the ford then crossed it, taking a pathway that would bring me to the village where I hoped a lawyer, a friend, a man I'd met hitchhiking called Pierre, would let me stay at his house for the night.

I came to a gathering of cherry trees where I had once sunbathed naked. Not far from there was the rocky path leading upward to the tiny village where Pierre's house sat perched on a cliffside. The approach was marked by large slabs of stone that met with the rock face into which were carved more steps that led into the citadel-like structure that was the town. I walked down cobblestone passages until I came to the lawyer's house, set below off the road and carefully made my way down a stairwell of flat stones. Once at the door, I knocked.

Thankfully Pierre was in and welcomed me. From my baggage he immediately divined the situation, assured me the ways of love were complicated and offered to host me for as long as need be so that I could continue to work in the small dental tool factory just outside of Nice and, above all, write – because he had read a short story I'd written and believed in me. In return I could teach him to play poker. He knew I was in the process of accumulating a bankroll for a weekend in Monte Carlo.

We had first met on my way hitch-hiking to work. When he discovered I lived nearby, he offered to drive me every morning if I met him at the village square. Like this, we had come to share certain details about our lives. We discussed politics, philosophy and novels, or else shared comfortable silences. He helped me at every turn with my French.

We sat at a large, roughly-hewn rectangular pine table in the kitchen drinking tea with bundles of herbs hanging from wooden beams overhead. Pierre again assured me that it wouldn't be a bother – I could stay as long as necessary. He enjoyed my company. It reminded him of when he was young and in a punk band. They all wrote the lyrics, he played the electric guitar and sometimes sang. He lived a wild life until he and his bandmates were in a serious road accident in which someone died. Pierre suffered a concussion. He began to realise he had become someone else and he vowed to devote his life to the law. It did not make complete sense, but for the first time he knew what his calling was. He obtained a degree specializing in human rights.

During the time I stayed with Pierre he revealed he had fallen very deeply in love with a woman who left him years ago, but that he was presently fending off his passions for a sister who lived in the nunnery. As time went on I felt his affections turn toward me but he hid it very well and never brought it blindly out into the open.

I didn't hear from Benoît for five months and went past our meeting point every day without fail. From the ramparts along the south side of the square I could see the Mediterranean and to the north, the peaks of the Alps – shining against the blue sky. I thought about going to Monaco, but decided against it. I had been experiencing the tell-tale signs of depression – lack of energy, lack of scent and smell, and a dullness of mind that terrified me. I could write, even though it was difficult and yielded around two paragraphs per three hours, the maximum amount of time I could concentrate. It took me about the same length of time to read five pages. Mornings until the late afternoon during the week were spent working in the factory while on weekends I would wander through the foothills, reading and writing at night.

Once Pierre and I visited Grasse, a medieval village perched in the hills with views of the Mediterranean that looked like something out of a fairy tale. It had seen the Romans, the Saracen raids, the machinations of courtly love and further back still, a prehistoric settlement. Perfume production began in the 17th century and Grasse went on to become the perfume capital of the world. The town had not been unknown to me. It was one of the places Camille and I marked on our map to visit and was one of the reasons I had come to the area. I had already explored the caves nearby, accessible by a hiking trail, and carried out a ritual, involving two dolls I made out of sticks, twine and felt, to draw her to me. The dolls were placed within a circle with the four directions marked out that corresponded to the appropriately coloured stones. A feather in between the doll that represented me and the one that represented Camille stood in the centre. Needless to say, I must not have performed the ceremony correctly because nothing out of the ordinary happened. I did not feel as though I had been able to communicate with her via thought transference and so was not able to call her to my location, which had been the aim of the exercise. I had failed like I failed at Altamira.

Pierre and I maintained a free and easy relationship. We occasionally got together for meals and rounds of no-limit poker. He taught me to play chess. One day I saw Benoît's truck on the corniche coming around the bend, the great vehicle edging slowly toward me and coming to a halt. It had been a bit more complicated than he'd foreseen. Gisele had been stolen by a heroin addict they were trying to rehabilitate. The said addict had driven off with all of his music equipment and everything he owned. He'd recovered the truck, but not much else. He had an envelope with a stack of cash in it and said we would need it for our new life together.

A year later, and here we were in a motel room in California, newlyweds, running from Las Vegas mobsters. Somehow, I was not surprised. I knew from the moment I saw Benoît that he'd take me to places no one else had.

"Madame Del Mar? *Tu penses à quoi, toi?*"

"Of the time we first met."

Ben was on his stomach, hands over his head, face tilted toward me – one dark, amber-green eye visible. He rolled over and reached for a cigarette on the bedside table, then propped himself up against the headboard, put his hand on my arm and lit his smoke.

"Baby, we're really in trouble now." I turned my face to his.

"From the moment we met, it was trouble." He smiled. "Trouble, it's the American Way, no? When in Rome –"

"I think trouble might be universal."

Ben blew smoke rings and gestured toward the mirror. "One thing I noticed about you, baby, you're very observant."

"The Chinese say there is always opportunity in times of crisis and danger."

"So, in fact, there is always opportunity, in good things and in bad."

"I hadn't thought of that. Maybe it has more to do with what I was explaining to you about possibility waves and probability curves applied to poker to increase the odds. How, when you focus, when you observe and concentrate, you make possibility waves that can turn into probability curves, rendering what you're fixated on more likely to happen.

"Thought turns into reality, into matter. You have to abandon reason and observe the world with pure will. Maybe this is what they meant. Being in danger makes one more attuned to the true reality of things."

Ben killed the cigarette in the ashtray. "Sometimes I 'ave no idea what you're talking about, baby, but I like to listen to your *théories*. Like anything is possible in this world of madness."

"Like you're going to spontaneously combust?"

He put his finger over my lips, then leaned over to kiss me, which led to another crazed session of sex. Afterward we lay there and I ran my fingers over Ben's back until he drifted off. I was unable to sleep so decided I would take a shower. I got up and drifted across the room to the bathroom on a high of sex and wasted adrenaline, then realised there wasn't any soap or shampoo, so I went back and lay down beside Ben until I finally fell asleep. We awoke hungry and got dressed. Benoît took cash out of the motel safe in the closet and counted it. "Baby, I'm sorry we can't go looking for your father now."

"I'm not sure I was ready to meet him." I lay on the bed.

"Look at me, baby, it's just you and me now and forever, and know this, I'm going to take care of you."

"I know you will." Now that we were being hunted down, it would be reckless to involve my father. He had left, or we had been taken from him, at age four. The last, brief encounter we had with him was at age six and deeply affected me. I saw him as a beacon and a riddle and wanted to find him but Camille maintained he had abandoned us, for whatever reasons, and had no interest in finding him. When I spoke of the happiness and love I felt in the few precious memories I had of him she would tell me that he was no longer that person, or that he would no longer be that person once he discovered what had been done to us. We would ultimately destroy him. It was best if we put him out of our minds. We had each other and that was enough.

Ben came to me and held my face in his hands that smelled of money. "I'm so sorry, baby. We'll find a way to contact him once we're settled and out of the country."

"Yes." I wondered whether fate had stepped in and caused the landslide that made reaching my father nearly impossible and potentially fatal. I should have listened to Camille.

Outside our room I stood and stared across the desert where the Red Rock Canyon glowed pink and ochre in the distance. I walked to the car while Ben made his way to the office, went inside and paid for another couple of nights. Through the windshield, I watched them converse, Ben and the young, squirrely-faced boy with the tattoo tear on his cheek we'd met the night before.

I looked at my reflection in the wing mirror. Camille. She was always there in the sun and in the shadows. It hit me like a dart to the solar plexus. Altamira. The scent went dead at Altamira. I had waited in the cave. As it turned out, there were two of them. One cave was the original, the other a replica made to protect it from the tourists. It was doubtful anything would be found in the simulacrum. Camille would have gone to the original. This meant I had to infiltrate and break into a World Heritage site unnoticed. Suffice to say, many days passed before I was successful, but more than time, it was luck and our espionage training under the tutelage of our childhood kidnapper and keeper, Dr V, which led to victory. And so, after eight days, I managed to slip in unnoticed. Each night I set up candles in a different location throughout the S-shaped caverns and expected Camille to appear to me out of the darkness.

I would lie down and stare up at the ochre-red coloured bison outlined in black, positioned as though they were tumbling from the sky, and focus on emptying my mind of thought. More often than not, before I fell asleep, the images of the animals became animated. The walls hummed so that my bones vibrated with the stones and I was let into what I can only describe as a chamber of dreams. There I lived among the men and women who had made the paintings. Day and night, asleep and awake, the lines began to blur. Symbols appeared out of the darkness. Geometric, phosphorescent forms made intricate patterns that appeared to me as angels and spoke in code. I understood that to find Camille I somehow had to access the knowledge these prehistoric people possessed. She had always surpassed me in ability. I felt the directives go in and knew that somewhere, somehow they were being deciphered, and that it would take time before they reached the shores of my immediate consciousness. A message in a bottle.

Many hours were spent making shadow puppets. The most heartbreaking was the amphibious brontosaurus which had been Camille's invention. After this time of fasting and meditation in the caves little demon faces began to appear floating in and out of the darkness, smirking at me. When I recovered from the delirium driven by an intense thirst that led me to cutting my wrist open with a Swiss Army knife and drinking, I knew it was time to move out. I was in over my neck.

The emotions felt like blood, rolling down my chest, down to the navel and I couldn't bear it. I saw her face lit up fireside, her cool smile as she cocked her head and laid her cards down, beating my three-of-a-kind with a straight. Camille in the forest, that day we found the cabin and broke in. And then I heard her voice (husky from a chain of sage smoking sessions) through the ventilation shafts recounting an Acoma legend of the Blue Corn Maiden until I fell asleep on the carpet.

I pressed my palms to the side of my head, looked for the cigarettes and was trying to light one when Benoît came back.

"Let's hit the road, Terror." He flicked the lighter to a flame. "You don't usually smoke cigarettes."

"Sometimes I do."

After twenty minutes or so we pulled off the highway into the parking area of a lone Fifties diner, all ribbed metal and glass. The counter ran most of the length of the lozenge-shaped space. Metal stools with red vinyl upholstery were riveted to the floor around it. The place was moderately busy. At the back sat a group of ravers tucked into a booth up against the large, panoramic windows, their legs stretched out in baggy pants with reflective cuffs, some with lollipops, others strung with pacifiers and Day-Glo coloured beads, candy bracelets on their wrists, eyes cat-like with possible ecstasy consumption. The two girls appeared quite spaced out, most notably the blonde with pink bangs who wore rabbit ears. A boy with buzz-cut auburn hair had his face painted into a skull and wore a Care Bears t-shirt, the other was naturally very blonde with nearly white eyebrows, and had dyed his hair blue. He had a face like a moon. Benoît clocked them before I did and led us on in their direction.

Candy ravers. I had heard of them. John, an American and former Marine I knew in Amsterdam from my commune days, described them to me once. He had summed them up with something like: "A bunch of fucked-up assholes dressed like Japanimation cartoons carrying glow sticks and children's backpacks filled with stickers, candy, and toys on them at all times. They like to suck on pacifiers and can pretty much be defined by their love of candy, not good candy, but jewellery candy, which they exchange with special candy kid kisses and handshakes as part of some bonding ritual." Their credo was Peace, Love, Unity, and Respect, or PLUR, an ideology which was also at the heart of the Amsterdam commune party people's unspoken manifesto. I didn't know enough about the Candy Ravers to make a truly informed comparison but with their worship of candy and Japanimation they surely differed from the Europeans who wore the mantles of the original 'hippy movement', were into veganism, healthy living, free love, yoga, ayahuasca and peyote rituals, Timothy Leary, Ram Dass, and Terence McKenna. As to what beliefs the Candy Kids subscribed to, I was in the dark, but they exuded a lackadaisical, California cool with a fatalistic air. Benoît and his people were yet another animal, probably closest in ideology to Chomsky's anarcho-syndicalism and more in the habit of taking cocaine and ketamine. However, in all groups I imagined there were those who would take whatever they could get their hands on. The Candy Raver movement had been only hearsay to me. And now, here some of them were before me.

Ben walked up to their table edge with me beside him. I smiled, waved, then excused myself and moved to the counter about four feet away and sat down on a stool so I could get the waitress's attention. Benoît stood behind and to the right of me, smoking a cigarette, engaging the candy ravers in conversation. "Hey, sorry to bother you boys and girls – " he winked at the glitter-faced blonde, then at the brunette with flourescent orange eye shadow. "I was just wondering, if dere was any techno, any 'ousy techno? Any tekky 'ouse? in da 'ouse?" He smiled, raised his arm, moving it to a four/four syncopated beat, glanced over at me still grinning, then turned back to them with his head cocked in a question.

Eight pairs of eyes – incredulous and round – stared back at Benoît and I. The boy with the moon face and cotton candy blue hair smiled. "House? Yeah, bro, we got house and techno till rainbows come out your ears tonight in Red Rock Canyon. Sweet party. You just come with us." His hand shot up for a high five and connected with Benoît's. The boy sat back and made a series of gestures with his hands that began with the peace sign, "PLUR, bro," then reached out and picked up a Pez dispenser out of one of the piles of candy on the table and proceeded to click and consume the fruit-flavoured tabs. "Dude, house is just good vibes. If you're looking for house, you've come to the right place. It brings us all together, you know. Raving is what it's all about. Anyone into the *music*, the vibe, you know – where's your accent from?"

"I'm from France. I deejay 'ouse with techno back dere. I play in underground, very underground parties, for the first times in Lyon, in warehouses, then all over France. Big parties. Teknivals. We just take over a field and put up a sound system. I love dose deep 'ouse grooves wit techno sounds and very, you know, those deep, dark melodies, that just get you right here." He put his fist to his chest.

The boy with the skull face stood up and hugged Benoît. "Yo, you're my brother from another mother, dude. Glad to have you on board."

The brunette raised her glittered arm and shot a peace sign in Benoît's direction. "Have a necklace, French man." She dangled a kryptonite-green beaded choker in the air, "I love your accent," then stood up and presented it to him, fastening it around his neck.

"You've gotta come, man. It's gonna be dope."

"What's all your names? I'm Ben, or Benoît. And 'ere's my wife, Genie."

I smiled and gave a little wave.

The blonde was Candy Pimp. She had become Candy Pimp only recently, before that she was Candy Kitten. The round-faced boy was either Baby Ruth or Pez because he had consumed nothing but Baby Ruths and Pez candy for two months and counting. The lanky boy with the skull face was Smudge. He could apparently smudge in and smudge out of reality. Candy Pimp testified to the phenomenon. Sometimes Smudge just vanished. "I'm straight edge, man. Naturally high on life."

Last was Ping Baby. She leaned in with her elbow on the table, cheek resting in the palm of her hand, and smiled. "I didn't get much sleep last night so forgive me if I'm foggy." Smudge divulged she had just won a junior table tennis championship in Las Vegas the night before. She sat back in the booth, tilted her head upward and explained that when she had taken her first E (just last week with a girl from school), someone had looked at her and shouted: "Ping! Baby!" at the moment of full climax on the dance floor, just as that first burst of ecstasy hit her bloodstream. She didn't look a day over fifteen. I wanted to tell her to wait, to go home, but maybe home was a barrel of monkeys, or worse, what did I know? We all have our reasons.

"Dude, he's a deejay. From France." Smudge patted Pez/ Baby Ruth on the back; she was lying inert, face down in a pile of gummy bears.

"Mate, maybe we need a medic." Ben gestured toward Baby Ruth.

"Naw, sailor, it's all right. It's just the candy. He's going intergalactic right now." Smudge asked for a cigarette, lit it and checked to see if Baby was still breathing. Then he hit him on the back again. "Dude, you're really missing this all here, this guy's a deejay from France."

Baby Ruth lifted his head and semi-opened his eyes. He picked a gummy bear off of his face, ate it and then continued to troll through the candy.

"You've done it now, Baby Ruth. I saw you eat that. You have to change your name to Gummy Bear." Candy Pimp giggled.

The newly christened Gummy cocked his hand into the shape of a gun and made a clicking noise as he pulled the trigger. "You got me."

Smudge told Gummy Bear he loved him and then turned to Benoît. "Do you, like, have any records here, bro? Cuz, like, maybe you could play."

"Yeah, I got maybe enough for a twenty-four-hour set. But not 'ere. It's at the motel."

"Candy kids, this is un-fucking-believable."

Candy Pimp nodded her glittered face, bunny ears quivering.

"You've *got* to play, man. I'm so amped. It'll be like *international*."

Ping Baby got up, hugged Benoît and gave him a stuffed penguin key chain.

"Dude, we're blessed. This is the bomb."

"You're the bomb. I'm honoured to meet all of you and accept your invitation. We haven't eaten in a while so, *bon appétit*, we must eat now. Check you in a bit." Ben bowed out and sat down beside me.

"I ordered us something to eat. Those ravers, they're called Candy Kids. Do you really think we should get mixed up with them right now?" I pleaded with my eyes the danger I felt.

"They seem 'armless to me."

"Harmless. You forgot the 'h'. It's just too risky to go back into Nevada for one thing, after everything that's happened and all, don't you think? Just, it seems like we should be figuring out what to do. I mean, shouldn't we be making our way to Reno if we're going to go back to Nevada, before the people in Vegas get to them about us? We could pick up an easy ten grand there. Then we can rave in Mexico." I had been considering our options and now didn't seem like the best time to go raving.

Benoît leaned back and shot smoke rings from his mouth. "Okay, well maybe we just wear disguises for the next one we hit. Go to the rave, rest, then take one down. That should be enough. We could be ready in twenty-four hours. Or not?" He took a drag from his cigarette and his eyes pinched up. "Don't we have enough? Let's not get greedy. We can stay low for a while. Take our honeymoon. Relax. We'll just swing by the motel, pick up my records. It's going to be *mortelle*."

I bit my lip and looked at him. I don't know how I slipped from the entirety of his face to deep inside the galaxy of his dark eyes, but inside, for an instant, there was the forest at night in winter lit up green and violet with the aurora borealis and the black outline of a deer.

The waitress came with two soda waters and our meal. I stared into the tall glasses, at the streaming bubbles racing to the top and bursting. "Okay, Tiger. Let's go." I kissed his cheek. The scent of him sent a warm charge through me. I wanted to keep kissing him.

"That's my girl." He lit a cigarette. "You won't regret this, *chérie*."

May 5th – 6th, Red Rock Canyons, Nevada

Out the rolled-down window, feverish with Mello Yello consumption, eyes tearing, face to the wind – the lone highway flung itself across the desert through a mountainous, rock-strewn landscape the colour of iron oxide.

We had deviated from reason which left me feeling unhinged and exposed yet with a mounting sense of power. Camille had said that when one had reached that place, the edge of terror and wonder, one had arrived. We were on the right path.

Benoît tapped his index finger on the steering wheel to a driving synthesizer drum, the off-beat hi-hat cymbals, icy through a spray of snares. Up ahead the candy ravers led the way in a white SUV. I noted how the sky seemed to be spiralling outward – as though sucked at a constant rate through a vortex, pulsating and expanding. A multilingual Russian novelist, poet, lepidopterist and chess composer once noted that the spiral is the spiritual circle: a circle set free. Had Camille and I spiralled out of the circle of life on Earth? Had that first cup of hemlock tea killed us? And then there were all of the other mishaps which could have resulted in the death of my body while my spirit lived on believing that the body was still there, like the phantom limb of an amputee. For all I knew I was my own hallucination. But in the end, what did it matter? Einstein had supposedly once said: "Logic will take you from A to B. Imagination will take you everywhere." As long as my imagination was intact, there were no limits. I could create meaning and purpose and that was enough.

Benoît stared ahead, both hands on top of the wheel, his form outlined against the red interior of the Cadillac with desert scenes flashing past. The road took a sudden bend through a rock ridge with a hole blasted through to form an archway. We slid close to the curving rock glowing tangerine in the sun and entered another realm.

Saguaro cacti stood like giant prehistoric idols in beams of roving red-orange light amidst agave stalks rising haphazardly, blooming with yellow lantern-shaped flowers. Outbursts of blue-eyed grasses and brush stood between aloe plants six feet in diameter – their ridged tendrils black against the sky.

"Woooohoooo!" Ben slung his arm out the window, throwing invisible lassos and kissed me on the cheek. "It's just you and me now, *mon bébé*."

The charge rose inside me like an electric serpent of smoke, coiling and uncoiling into ecstatic shapes. I bit my lip and looked at him. "*Moi aussi, mon bébé*. Anywhere and anything with you." Ben leaned in and kissed me on the temple.

We were getting deeper into the canyons, behind the SUV with the candy ravers inside, turning off the highway onto a dirt road, tyres throwing up red clouds of dust, which spooled over the windshield. Ben held back and let the others gain more distance. We rolled slowly, the chassis rocking from side to side over the rough terrain. Soon the view from the windshield was obscured by a layer of dirt and we had to put our heads out the side windows to navigate, looking for rocks all the while, continuing like this behind the SUV, losing proximity until the taillights disappeared. We followed the dirt road another five miles or so with Saguaro cacti in flower all around until we came to the edge of a mesa.

Ben angled the car between outbursts of brush and parked. I opened the glove compartment, took out a pair of binoculars, then exited the car and went to the canyon edge.

Pin prickles went up the back of my neck. I felt perhaps something like Judy Garland just landed in Oz and noted that in the film, behind the scenes, the Munchkin actors were purported to have had countless orgies while Garland was pumped with amphetamines. Down below could only be described as Nature in a State of Delirium. Through the sights, swarms of wild-eyed, ecstatic, half-naked, day-glowed, costumed and painted people danced helter-skelter, some spitting fire, others juggling fireballs on chains, all united by the pulse of the beat emanating from the stack of speakers underneath an open circus tent. Maybe a hundred feet from the tent opening was a tree with a body hanging from it. I had never seen party people dancing like this in my entire life. Not even the Americans I had known in Europe. The fluidity of their movement was supernatural.

I got back into the car and passed Ben the binoculars – he took them, ran his hand along the dash, sat back, then leaned over me and opened the glove compartment looking for a new pack of cigarettes. He took one out, tapped it on the top of the box and lit it, his elbow leaning out the window. He had a good poker face, almost as impenetrable as Camille's. A chain of smoke rings shuttled out of Benoît's mouth. One drifted above my head like a halo. "You're my angel, baby." He then picked up the binoculars, and peered through them. "I hope I get to play some music. Promise me one thing, baby, you just stay close to me when we go down there."

"I will." I sat back, played with the radio and watched him smoke. He put the binoculars on the dash and stared ahead, becoming more and more remote – a distant star. I didn't want to disturb him, snuff his flame out. People are like fires, they need space and air to breathe and reach their potential.

I couldn't find anything on the radio, it was all static, country and western tunes, religious talk shows, more static until I heard the first chords of Bob Marley's 'Stir it Up' and started to move to the music. Ben turned to me with a glint in his eye. "Baby, take off that dress."

I slipped the sundress over my head and sat half-naked in front of him. Then, there was no stopping it. Kisses degenerated into biting. Ben protected my back from the steering wheel. When it was finally, categorically, the end,

Ben lifted me off of him and set me down on the seat where I got dressed as Ben smoked.

Again I was plagued by doubt. I could not help but reassess the hare-brained idea of crossing state lines back into Nevada – into a situation that could potentially end in our arrest, trial and incarceration for armed robbery and kidnapping if the law caught wind of the brouhaha in the desert. We should have been on the road, calculating our next hit before the entire gaming area caught on to us, then hightailing it out of North America on the first flight available. Maybe to Colombia or Peru. We could find the Desana and take ayahuasca and remotely locate Camille. Maybe she was already with the tribe, sending me mental messages. But I'd promised Ben. I'd said Yes. No turning back or we'd become pillars of salt.

We stepped out of the car. Ben went about cleaning the dirt from the windshield with a rag from the trunk, water and washer fluid.

The site was idiosyncratic and awe-inspiring; the kind of place generations of desert tribes must have come to perform rituals in devotion to the spirits. Cream and orange Aztec sandstone walls rose several hundred feet from the canyon floor, cut into a cove-like structure by glaciers and wind so that it made a sunken oasis with the river running through it at the site of the rave. Green lowlands spread out for miles below with the river glinting blue and violet, vein-like and seeming to disappear into the horizon. Above, clouds were lit up like fire opals.

The four/four beat of the music from the rave below drifted up from the canyon lip. Ben did a three-sixty around the Cadillac, crouching, inspecting for damage. He took out his Dictaphone, looked at me, put his index finger to his mouth and recorded the sound of a cactus wren before we started down the road to the canyon floor. Benoît squinted, pulled me close and kissed me on the top of my head. "Don't stray from me." He locked the car and we found a trail downward with boulders marking the way.

The sun was almost down. We approached the kaleidoscopic scene and walked into it. Sage smoke hung in the air mixed with wafts of patchouli, rose, clothing detergent, perspiration, the bitter scent of cocaine and ecstasy, as well other odours too numerous to name. The force of the music coming from the four towers of sound made my flesh and bone vibrate with it and I again thought of the Hal-Saflieni Hypogeum in Malta.

Two half-naked, painted girls skipped past us, one with fairy wings, the other with an M16 squirt rifle. We pressed along and found ourselves at the heart of the rave, in the centre of the great, dancing, carousing mass, all moving to the off-beat rhythms, cymbals, spray of hi-hats through a deep, dark house track. Dry ice smoke hissed and filtered out from the edges of the speaker towers.

It became apparent that the hanging man was an effigy of Uncle Sam with a pile of sticks underneath it. Not far away a girl danced with fireballs on chains while a circle of people smoked, danced and took drugs around her. And so we had entered a place of lawlessness and civil disobedience populated by worshippers of beats in the rawness of Nature with MDMA for communion wafers.

A guy with an incongruous smile and a trucker cap came running by and sprayed the crowd with a water pistol – Benoît and I included. The music continued to hold me with its sorcery. I danced and let my mind run. It seemed the plan was to hold the area by occult means – it appeared to be a revolution of sorceresses and sorcerers. It soon became apparent that there was something other than water in the gun, most likely LSD, or some kind of derivative. When taken through the eyes, the effect of lysergic acid is almost immediate. I felt Ben's hand slip away as the kaleidoscope turned. Random pieces of reality (forget-me-nots, a pipe, a harmonica, an axe, a helmet, et cetera) fell past with a radioactive glow. I found myself speeding through a telescope. Welcome to the Mysteries (applause), to the land of the Red Queen (peals of shrill laughter). Then a voice whispered: "Peace is a snare. War is a snare. Change is a snare." And finally: "Permanence is a snare." It was clear that this life was over. There was no turning back. I was being hurled through the tunnels of death.

May 6th – 7th, Red Rock Canyons, Nevada

The next thing I knew I was a speck of consciousness, or more like a nanoprobe in the flotsam and jetsam of space, my movement prohibited by some centrifugal force fixing me in orbit around a gigantic, pulsating black hole that spoke to me with a voice full of resonance, looping over again and again: *This is your reality for all eternity.* I panicked and knew I had landed in a sphere of hell.

After a while, out of the void, Bruce Lee spoke to me: "Notice that the stiffest tree is most easily cracked, while the bamboo or willow survives by bending with the wind." I bent and surrendered to my fate; the black hole vanished.

More than anything, I was struck by the light – radiance pouring in from all corners. Soon after my vision became like a bee's with eight identical images containing a semi-circle of brightly coloured individuals seated around me in rainbow sheets of sunlight. It seemed as though an incredible amount of time had elapsed and I had travelled very far.

This insect 'video feed' of the people then took up one large frame to compose the totality of my field of vision.

These creatures were very humanlike but their eyes were huge and round, their skin pale, like grubs, masticating. I tried to speak. No sound came out at first. I looked down and realised I had a body. There was a key chain toy in my hand – a penguin. Later the people kept repeating they'd given me the penguin and thought I was dead. They made me drink orange juice and tried to get me to eat some candy.

I got up (light as a ghost), knowing there was somewhere I had to be, someone I had to find, but not knowing who and seeing the face of a boy with auburn hair, his face painted to look like a skull. He had special powers that could possibly lead me to the person I needed to find. *Camille*. Her name was *Camille*.

A sylphlike girl with dreadlocks mixed through her white blonde hair walked toward me, pulled me close and whispered huskily into my ear:

Vindum, vindum
vef darraðar,
þann er ungr konungr
átti fyrri!
Fram skulum ganga
ok í fólk vaða,
þar er vinir várir
vápnum skipta.

I had heard the incantation before. Dr V had made us memorize it. It was ancient Norse, chanted during the rituals in the burials of chieftains where a slave girl is submitted to sexual rites before being sacrificed. The chief's body is placed in a ship while the slave girl is sent from tent to tent where she has sex with warriors and traders who each tell her that they are doing it for the love of the dead chieftain. Then she is taken to a tent raised on the ship where six men have sex with her again before she is strangled and stabbed. The purpose of it all was to make her a vessel for the transmission of life force to the deceased chief.

Things were coming back to me, words like little poisoned arrows soaked in the rotting milk voice of Dr V. He had taught us many incantations and rituals, often repeating to us how there was great power in blood and procreative fluids because the mixing of all of that DNA, all the life force with the biophotons, resulted in a powerful alchemy. A transformation occurred. One became immortal. The thought chilled Camille's blood and mine. If Dr V became immortal the world was doomed. Murderous plots began to hatch between us. Something had to be done before he stumbled upon the exact formula.

This "immortality" was linked to the concept of Antiterra, a theory Nabokov had (perhaps unwittingly, according to Dr V) stumbled upon, channelled during one of his trances when he wrote *Ada or Ardor*. Apparently if one were to meet one's anti-self and touch, one would be completely annihilated in a flash of light. (Camille and I later confirmed the theory in Stephen Hawking's *A Brief History of Time*.)

Camille had been barely able to breathe from the excitement, her face stricken, index finger gesturing discreetly toward the door, while we excused ourselves and ran up the stairs. She was hardly able to contain herself, because Kafka, in his blue octavo notebooks, wrote: "There is nothing besides a spiritual world; what we call the world of the senses is Evil in the spiritual world, and what we call Evil is only the necessity of a moment in our eternal evolution. One can disintegrate the world by means of a very strong light." She was convinced that Antiterra contained this Light. And that it held a key to immortality.

Something soft hit my calf followed by a jab like a large hypodermic needle. Adrenaline kicked in. A feral scream scrawled out of me, raw and electric in my throat as the reptile slipped away.

People came toward me.

I collapsed and watched myself become a corpse piece by piece. Benoît's face came through a blur of red, got closer and eclipsed the sky.

May 9th, Monte Carlo Medical Center, Utah

My insides felt chemical – like my veins were running antifreeze. The cold gas from the mask burned my throat. A metal object pressed into my cornea. Somehow, I tore the mask off. A nurse came to my bedside, bringing with her the pungent stench of putrefying goat's lungs and formaldehyde. She hung over me, her pale, powdered face searching mine and slipped the mask back on. Cold water filled my ear canals and trickled down the back of my throat. I felt like I was going to suffocate. I couldn't move my limbs. Doctors congregated around me.

"It's a roll of the dice."

"A waste of life. Nasty, snake bites."

"Her resemblance to the actress in that German vampire movie is unnerving."

"She looks like Snow White, after she ate the poison apple."

"Let's rock and roll, boys."

My head felt bolted like a calf in a slaughterhouse. Everything went black.

*

Needles slid out of my veins. The oxygen mask came off of my face. Ben unhooked me from the machines. I was in his arms and then in a wheelchair, rolling down brightly lit corridors that smelled of sick, of disease, ammonia bleach and glove rubber. My eyes were weighted like a doll's. When I moved my head I heard and felt a metal bead rolling back and forth where my spine met my cranium. A throbbing pain came from the holes in my leg.

We sailed out through the automatic doors. The air was soft and the breeze felt good, as we moved across the parking lot to the Cadillac where Benoît picked me up and buckled me into the passenger side. He kissed me on the side of my head. "Don't worry, baby."

Benoît pulled out nice and slow and got us onto the boulevard. Rows of giant palms slipped past. He popped the cap off a Coca-Cola bottle with his teeth and handed it to me. The bubbles burned my throat. It was good to be on the road. The Cadillac moved smoothly like a boat floating past carnival-lit, whimsical cities on the river banks at night. A worn and pockmarked temple slipped by like an enigma. Saturn devouring his son rose up behind the silhouettes of buildings in thick, inky clouds of smoke and obscured the starry sky.

I was not the same girl I used to be. Somewhere in the dull woolpack of morphine there was something aberrant, something that hadn't been there before, or something that had just come to the surface to be revealed.

"You've woken up just in time, sleeping beauty." Ben caressed the side of my face. "You're a cat." He stared back at the road. "I knew they were full of shit. You're not going to die on me are you, Terror? They don't know what you're made of. You're like a cat with nine lives, baby. I've got to admit, I thought you were being a little Looney Tunes when you told me you and your sister might be immortal but now, it's beginning to sound more like the truth." Soon we hit the highway, out into the desert, where we could breathe easier, the road skating eastward under a dome of stars with mountains in the distance and cacti flickering by like Rorschach inkblots.

Benoît stared ahead, his hand on mine. "I'm going to take care of you, baby. *Merde*, what the fuck is that?" He leaned up on the wheel and sat back again. "I thought I saw a brontosaurus." He laughed and reached for a cigarette. "*Bien foutu* that LSD. *Bien foutu*. Clack! Just about as terrible as you, Terror. Come over here." He put his arm around my shoulder, pulled me close to him and whispered, "Those demons will strangle on their own dust. What goes around comes around, baby. They'll get a good dose of fear," he looked up at the rear-view mirror and then back at the road ahead, "in a handful of ether. That's for sure. They said you were dead, they wanted to sell your organs. Well, baby, that isn't going to happen with me around." I watched him change gears. White ash from his cigarette fell to the floor. "You've got at least nine lives, *ma chérie*, the acid, the viper. *Allez*." He gave a slight nod to the road ahead and then kissed me gently on the cheek and began to sing: "*Happi-ness is a waaarm gun, happi-*

ness..." He made his hand in the shape of a pistol: "*Bang. Bang. Shoot. Shoot.* We're just going to drive a bit further on, away from the crime. Go over state lines and find a nice motel where we can relax. Maybe I'll drive all night..." Ben drove while I half slept up close against him with my ear on his chest, listening to his heart beating.

"Nature ... talks in symbols." My voice was not my usual voice; it came from some dark, far-off place, flickering with the darkness and light of fairy tales and marauding, glowing orbs. Joy, rapture, wonder, terror, flickered through "me" (a concept too incomprehensible to decipher in the immediate present) as what I had become stared out to the desert highway, expanding and decaying through the windscreen. Eons went by. Every word – and every thought – allowed access to an infinite pool of meaning that was too complex and vast for my mind to process. The ashtray was open. There were piled joint ends, like crumpled moth cocoons, or lives burnt out, inked with ash. Larvae of dread boiled up in my gut. Tiny white butterflies broke through the cocoons and spilled out of the ashtray, buoying me up with delight.

"One could go mad from one ashtray."

"I know what you mean, baby."

May 9th, Southern Utah to Lake City environs, Colorado

We drove through the night. Thunder rumbled over the desert. Dry lightning lit the sky up violet and green. I was feverish, my vision blurred at times. Ben pulled into a motel parking lot. I stayed in the car while he went to reception to get the keys. "I'll be right back, baby. Just hold tight." I thought I might vomit so I opened the car door. A breeze came by and offered some relief but then the air began to thicken with an electrical charge.

Thunder cracked like a sawed-off shotgun blast, rattling the car. I could see and feel myself from all angles, three hundred and sixty degrees, like a roving camera. The concrete buildings, the asphalt and all the rocks lying around began a high-pitched humming, each one in a different tone with a slow, inevitable rhythm that intensified. Violet branches of lightning lit up the sky. An uncomfortable charge built up in me. All my hairs stood on end. The weight of it and the humming became unbearable. My mind began to crack. Thunder struck again soon after the lightning hit. As soon as it had come the drone and the pressure phased out. I sat and concentrated on my breathing.

A flag flapped in the wind across the highway. A tabby cat wandered across the parking lot. "Kitty, kitty. *Minou, minou, minou.*" I called to it as though in a dream and held out my hand. The cat ran toward me with a little bell jingling around its neck. My head filled with a warm, electric ooze that pushed and pulsated and ran down through me as I watched a violet jet of current ejaculate through my outstretched arm and lock on to the cat like a heat-seeking missile, tossing the animal several feet into the air and causing it a considerable amount of pain before it fell to the ground, crackling with blue light. My first instinct was to go to the cat. I pulled myself up with the door. The fever sent shivers through me. Everything was a blur. I moved like a diver navigating the ocean floor. Before I made it to the animal Ben came out with the keys.

"Baby, what are you doing?"

"The cat." I made a motion to point but pulled my hand back.

He turned, saw the cat lying there motionless and went to it. "It's not dead." Ben stroked its fur. "It's been shocked or something. Hit by a car. Did you see it?"

"It was me."

"What?"

"An electric bolt flew out of my hand."

"Okay, well, you go to the room while I bring the cat into the reception and see if they can help." He got up to hand me the keys.

"Throw them to me."

"Why?"

"I don't want you to get shocked, like the cat."

He didn't argue, threw them to me and took off his shirt to wrap around the animal and walked back to the office. I walked past the Cadillac without shutting the door then stared at the key for a while, trying to make out what number it was. My eyes stung. There remained a residual charge that hummed through me. Getting inside the room was potentially risky, due to the electrical current surging through me. I put the key in the lock. There was a jolt but not enough to keep me from getting the door open. I stepped inside, put the key on the night table, then sat on the bed too afraid to move until Ben returned, staring at the door, praying I had not killed or maimed the cat.

Had the snake poison *done* something to me? Camille and I learned of medicine men using snake venom for its magical, occult properties but had never been able to get our hands on any. There were occasions when we had been able to psionically control the weather with our incantations, sacrifices, and ceremonies – however, channelling enough ambient electromagnetism to generate a blast that would throw a cat into the air was far beyond our capabilities. At the time we had been studying texts from the ancient Bön tradition of Tibet as well as reading social anthropological studies on Native American medicine men. We once called a hailstorm that knocked Dr V unconscious, but not long enough to make our escape.

During the practice of these meditations an electromagnetic charge (similar to the one I was presently experiencing, but at another frequency) would build up between Camille and me. At times it was palpable even to bystanders. On occasions we had even become invisible.

It was clear that the charge had something to do with all of these unusual happenings. Dr V attributed our powers to the pills, injections, cognitive behavioural therapies and radiation treatments as part of a programme to genetically enhance us. We were to be the next models in human evolution with heightened intelligence and physical prowess, immune to radioactive materials, ultimately able to consume such material and use it for food. We were not to speak of this to anyone, however. Everything was very hush, hush. It was one of the reasons why we had to use different names at school and with the townspeople.

Dr V always used to say that if you use a blunt saw to cut wood you won't be able to compete with someone using a razor sharp one. The nature of your study and the nature of your practice influence the outcome. He made us wear electromagnetic helmets to put us in an 'autistic-like state' so that we could concentrate on the subject at hand all day long without tiring. It had been found effective by the military in accelerating soldiers' learning, according to the doctor.

The End of Times was nigh. Soon the earth would be covered with dangerous levels of radioactivity. Our lives revolved around this certainty. It was the same one that had the Born Again Christians, Mormons and such stocking their basements and bomb shelters, only Dr V's vision was more detailed and cohesive. He concluded that aside from the certainty of the Apocalypse, all organised religions were 'idiotic' and the followers had 'mental deficiencies'.

"People who end up Jehovah's Witnesses," he used to say, "have a mental deficiency I refer to informally, but most aptly, as 'the inability to call BS'. When I study the Bible I call BS left and right. When a Jehovah's Witness or fundamentalist Christian studies the Bible they believe every word of it. In short, those people are deficient."

Ultimately, all of our teachers and all the people in the town were living in ignorance. Dr V had superior knowledge. Somehow all of this was connected to a mission that would take place on the eve of our eighteenth birthday after which we would go to the Monte Carlo casino, take the house down and receive further instructions, instructions which may or may not have existed at that point in time. The event never took place. Circumstance, opportunity, a bottle of perfume and a swarm of killer bees changed our fate.

Camille and I spent many nights with a flashlight under the sheets reading comic books. The worlds depicted in them were similar to our own in many ways. We felt a special affinity with one character, a girl, who bent light using moisture in the air to manipulate the fog and mist, thus allowing her to become transparent, and later, once she honed her powers, invisible. Camille and I had noticed that in certain moments during our meditations we would be popped into a hologram world where everything, including ourselves, was transparent, our differentiations delineated by rainbow shimmers. Other times we became invisible with no control whatsoever, disappearing and re-appearing in plain sight, in front of witnesses, on multiple occasions. We learned very quickly that things which shock people are either brushed under the carpet, or reacted violently against. Our ability to become invisible alarmed Dr V at first, but then excited him.

My thoughts imploded on themselves. The fever overtook me. I lay there flickering on, off, on, off, my eyes burning, everything taking on a holy glow. I heard Camille, singing an old popular song from a bygone era: "*You are my sunshine, my only sunshine; you make me happy when skies are grey; you'll never know dear, how much I love you; please don't take my sunshine away...*" It was a message. When I opened my eyes, Ben was beside me. He stroked my hair. I was ice cold and ice hot. Ben wiped my forehead with a wet cloth and made me take sips of water. The carpet burst into flame, which began to crawl up the walls. Camille came and stood in the midst of it all, her hair dancing in the rising heat, beckoning to me with a bird tibia in her hand, like ones we used to play the bone throwing game with. I got up to follow her but Ben took my wrist and everything disappeared – Camille, the flames, the sound, the heat, all was gone. Nothing had burned. I lay on the bed, my head soaked in sweat, his hand holding mine.

"Baby, you're burning up." He held a cool, wet washcloth to my forehead, then took it off when it became warm and threw it onto the back of a chair. Benoît slid down to lay next to me and smelled of copper and violets. I listened to him breathing and to the beat of his heart as he fell asleep. I lay and watched our shadows on the green wall through a sphere of yellow light cast by the bedside lamp and struggled to remember the chain of events that had led us to the motel room. I realised I was still feverish and bit the bullet, trying to stay as still as possible, wishing I could crawl out of my skin. I fell in and out of consciousness.

Ben woke up and gave me more quinine and laudanum he'd found in some backwater pharmacy. When the ray of the light of dawn came in through the curtains I knew that sleep had been lost to me.

May 10th-11th, Southern Utah, Lake City environs, Colorado

Even with my fever we couldn't stop. We had to get into the mountains and lay low. Ben had made me a comfortable nest of blankets and pillows from the motels on the back seat and given me a bottle of water. After many hours on the road, the fever finally broke. Ben stopped to get us something to eat and we ate in the car. As I began to gather strength I realised the strange current had not left me entirely; it had changed to static electricity. The hairs all over my body stood on end, prickly with the static charge that stuck to me like a nightdress. My hair was becoming a bird's nest.

Out of the corners of my eyes, along the roadsides, I kept seeing Camille. She was trying to communicate something. We were getting closer. Benoît pulled the Cadillac onto a used car lot. "We're gonna change cars, baby. I'd say four-wheel drive. So we can get up into our honeymoon hideaway." We cruised the lanes of parked cars, eventually stopping in front of a white Mitsubishi Montero.

"This is it, Terror – our new ride." Ben kissed me on the cheek, stroked my hair and smiled at me before reversing back to the front of the auto shop through the lanes of parked cars. He turned the engine off, turned to me and put his hand to my cheek, then tapped the dash, got out of the car and walked across the lot. It struck me that he had touched me and nothing had happened. No charge. I watched him through the dusty windshield until he disappeared into the office where he struck a deal with the salesman, most surely gave a false name and came out with the keys. I said a silent goodbye to the Cadillac. Ben pulled the Montero around and then quickly arranged everything into the back of it. We hit the road.

I lifted the bandage on my leg and saw the holes were the size of two cigarette burns, then put the dressing back again. The serpent would most likely leave its mark on me. I threw my dress off to reduce the build-up of static charge, one of the few tips I remembered from Dr William J. Beaty's article on 'electric people' entitled: "Humans and Sparks: The Cause, Stopping the Pain" from a medical journal in our childhood library. Ben rolled down the power windows. "Baby, please. We're in the daylight here, high up, all the truckers –"

I put my dress back on. I had to grin and bear it. The sensation of being high on the road was comforting, but otherwise lonely and inhibiting, separated from Ben by a compartment with a worn stress reliever pig superglued to the top of it, pinned to the seat by a seatbelt more like a straitjacket. I missed the room to move freely, to lie down, sprawl my legs out and nuzzle up to Ben while he was driving as I'd done in the Cadillac. The mood had changed. Gone were the ample, cream leather seats lined with black appointments, gone the dash with dark, fake wood panelling, the elegant ashtray, gone the big, round cockpit gauges, and the steering wheel, all the cream leather and shiny silver metal, gone. The Montero had a tilt inclinometer gauge pod stuck to the centre of the dash with three liquid-filled bubbles for each gauge, the centre one with a red danger line to warn you when you were going too far off-kilter, which seemed beside the point, but added to the whimsical effect. In front of me a plastic handlebar rose out of the dash mould. It reminded me of a log ride at Disney World, one in which Camille and I had gotten stuck with Dr V as part of a 'family holiday', and had to listen to the screeching, tinny notes of "It's a Small World After All" until I thought I would vomit. I lost consciousness. Everything went polka dots. I came to in the hotel bed with Camille's face close to mine, whispering: "Don't worry, I've been protecting you."

We passed through more desert towns, driving into the night (through higher and higher altitudes under the stars). Ben pulled into a motel, corralled me into a cold bath and kept dumping in ice to bring the new bout of fever down. I lay on the bed having visions and nightmares while Ben spooned me the bitter tinctures of quinine and laudanum.

In the morning we had to move on. The bed rest had given me strength. I remembered a case similar to mine, one I'd read about in a medical journal from the 1920s, chronicling an outbreak of botulism at a prison. Somewhere in Upstate New York. Sixty-four inmates got sick. Along with the food poisoning they'd become charged like electric eels. The men shot glowing rays from their fingers and shocked whoever touched them. The more severe the poisoning, the higher the charge. When the prisoners recovered they went completely back to normal. There was hope. When I explained it all to Ben he looked dumbfounded, reached for a cigarette, and then put his eyes back on the road.

We stopped at the next possibility for lunch – a country store restaurant – and ordered something to eat. I felt my eyelids droop and found myself gripping onto the booth in an effort to hold myself down – my body felt light as helium. The lights were too bright. I could feel them and the bright colours, such as the red upholstery that covered the booths and stools, grinding against my eyes, their frequencies playing on my nervous system. I put on a pair of sunglasses.

Ben scarfed down his steak and eggs while I sipped on a Cherry Coke and stared at the road map laid out in front of us. It looked like a miniature terrain with mountain ranges and valleys and made me think of Borges' fable about the Imperial Map. The Imperial Cartographers were so faithful to the territory they were charting that the map eventually covered every inch of the Empire. In the end only tatters of the map remained, strewn about the desert.

"You should eat more, Terror." Ben held out his fork with a piece of steak on it.

I shook my head – 'no' – took a cigarette out of the pack on the table and lit it.

"You're not recovered from the fever or the snake bite, baby. Don't smoke."

I wanted to tell him that I was smoking because we were made to smoke, that we have nicotine receptors in our brains, that shamans in places like Peru use it to cure just about anything, et cetera, but I was in a state of exhaustion and pleaded with my eyes not to worry.

"Baby, you need to eat, not smoke."

I held tears back.

"Sorry, Terror." He put the meat on my plate. I picked it up with my fingers. It was greasy and felt like a foreign object in my mouth, still, I chewed.

I waved my hand over a spoon. Static ripped through my head as electric blue sparks shot out of my fingertips. I put my hands under the table. I felt like I might disappear in a flash of photons. The cigarette was nauseating. I pushed it away. Ben killed it in the ashtray.

Ben made a motion to reach out to me, remembered my anxiety about the charge, and instead rested his arm on the table.

"I can't wait till we get off the road." I closed my eyes and focused on my breathing. The place where the snake bit me throbbed.

"We will. Soon. Please, baby, just eat a bit and then we're out of here."

"I'm doing the best I can." Yes, that was all I wanted – to get up into the mountains with my Venus Acid Boy, find a cabin, and try to figure out what was happening to me. Solve it. Solve the riddle. Solve all of them and find Camille.

"Listen." Ben looked serious. "You need to eat more, Terror. If you don't eat, then that's when you're really going to disappear and I can't live without you so at least finish your eggs." He turned his head slightly toward the counter and then back to me. "Maybe you could drink a milkshake. Or eat a piece of pie?" He motioned to the waitress – Lucy, according to the name tag pinned to her white-smocked, egg-shell blue uniform – and caught her eye. She nodded and smiled brightly, then took her sweet time walking over to us from behind the counter across the black and white chequered floor along a steadfast trajectory that landed her at our table edge, pen at the ready. Ben ordered a strawberry milkshake. "Say, where would you recommend going for a honeymoon in the area? Somewhere remote and tranquil."

She answered with a far-off look in her eyes (chewing gum): "The Alpine Loop's nice. People come from all over the country to see it."

"Sorry, what was that?" Ben turned his good ear toward Lucy, fork raised and at an angle.

"The Alpine Loop. Just follow the signs. I've never been there but plenty of people come through here, aiming to go there. It's supposed to be real pretty, with all the mountains and wild flowers. It's not too far." She held her notepad closer, raised an eyebrow, gently exposed the inside of her tattooed wrist, then put her hand on the table, leaning in so close I could smell the Ivory soap on her skin. "You're not from around here. Where're y'all from?"

"I'm French."

"Wow, French, huh? I like your accent." A smile crept over her face, eyes smouldering, pen bobbing.

"Well, we French, we love the American accent." He put the fork down and wiped his mouth with a napkin.

"Hey, I've got some friends I'd like you to meet. They're planning on going to Paris in two weeks. Do you mind if I bring them over?"

Benoît smiled politely and winked. "Not at all." Lucy sauntered off.

I had been observing Lucy. She employed some of the same techniques a posse of venomous, cherubim-cheeked high school girls had used on Camille and me which ultimately resulted in mental confusion and a draining of energy that Dion Fortune described so aptly in her work *Psychic Self-Defence* (Camille had insisted the book was a must; we did a 'mission impossible' and stole it from Dr V's private library). Here we learned the basic ins and outs of 'psychic vampirism'. These 'Vamps', as we called them (Dr V was also a Vamp, an extremely high functioning one), lull you into a false sense of security, as Lucy had done with her sugary voice and submissive showing of wrists, miming the host, mimicking their voice tones just slightly off-kilter, so that it takes someone who is truly observant to notice. Then, once they have you close they bury their head in, like a tick.

"What are you thinking about, Terror?"

"Vampires." I whispered across the table, "She's one of them. Lucy. Have you noticed?"

"My God, Terror. No, no I hadn't."

My eyes widened. Ben's sparkled. Blood pumped in my ears.

Ben took out his Dictaphone and put it on the table. "Now that you mention it –" He got a wolfish kind of grin. "Let's see if we can pick up any evidence of vampiric interference."

Ben had taken the ball and run with it. His indulgence thrilled me. I felt raised out of the feverish haze and it hit me that in that moment I was like Camille, when she positively glowed with some far-fetched idea and I would suspend disbelief and play along while she went off on Diego Rivera and his cannibalism, the implications of biophotons in DNA, Pleiadians, ancient Vedic texts, Kafka, et cetera, and I felt the switch, like I'd seen so many times in Camille's eyes, shimmering into dark pools of mischievous laughter. She was here. She was with me, speaking through me. "It even smells like Vampires." My heart leapt. Then I noticed my nose had started to bleed.

"Terror –"

I put a napkin to my face and pinched my nose.

"Baby, you know what, let's just get out of here. Drive as far as we can and find our honeymoon spot."

"I concur."

Lucy was right on cue. She came strolling up to us with little bobs of the hips back and forth, trying to hypnotize us, flanked by two men, sure to appear as two bright, blipping green lights on even the most unsophisticated of Gaydar, one holding a VHS camcorder, filming as they approached. It seemed they wanted us to know, loud and clear, that they were homosexual. It was suspicious. Ben motioned to me with his eyes in the direction of the Dictaphone. Lucy put the strawberry milkshake down in front of me and winked.

The blond, who I shall call Sabertooth (built like a WWF fighter, tight camel-coloured leather pants, open lumberjack shirt, a golden amulet and golden mat of chest

hair, big beard, crazy hair, shiny teeth), sat down next to
me and aimed his camera at us while the other portly one
with a dark, oily, slicked-backed coiffure – Wolverine –
edged up next to Ben, practically breathing down his neck.
They never introduced themselves. The dark one had a
lithe power. Despite being rather squat and slightly rotund
he was shifty, fluid. I could see from the way he moved,
the gestures he made, the words he used like a probe,
that he harboured a psychotic viciousness which knew few
bounds. He would have attacked a man ten times his size,
as wolverines in the wild have been known to do, dropping
onto bears' backs from the treetops and successfully
chasing them from their dens for a carcass.

After the usual chit-chat and informalities Sabertooth
asked Ben if I was his girlfriend. When he told them I
was his wife, Wolverine asked him if he'd ever had 'fuck
buddies', repeating the term three times (a magical number,
like a hypnotist snapping his fingers).

Ben covered the camera lens with his hand. "If you're
going to disrespect me and my wife with your obscene
questions you can go elsewhere." He finished smoking his
cigarette, took a gulp of coffee, then bit into a chocolate-
frosted doughnut, ripping it apart with his teeth, devouring
it in seconds. The conversation did not continue on that
path. Ben motioned to Lucy in the distance (smiling behind
the counter, coffeepot in hand) for the cheque.

Lucy took her sweet time. Finally, she came by with a
slice of cherry pie she said was for Benoît because she'd
promised him a piece earlier, the same recipe that had won
best in the region for eleven consecutive years (an outright

lie, she never mentioned cherry pie). It was the last piece of prize-winning pie and no one but Ben was to touch it. She put it on the table, insisting to both me and them and to herself that only Ben was to eat the piece of pie. It was a big deal. A big thing. Ben slid the pie to me from across the table. "At least take one bite, baby, then we can hit the road." Benoît picked up a fork. "Does anyone else want any pie?" He said this with an even, deadpan tone, motioning to Sabertooth and Wolverine.

"No thank you," Sabertooth declined, his camera still filming but pointed out the window.

Then it was Wolverine's turn. "No. None for me."

I ate two bites of pie with difficulty. Ben put his fork down, still chewing. Sabertooth looked across the table at Wolverine, then at Benoît. "Can we have a bit each on second thought?"

Benoît showed no argument. "Of course." He pushed the plate over to them. The whole thing was a test. The beginning was the setup and the second part was a yardstick to measure his will.

Now what I'm about to describe is the worst thing done and it was carried out by Lucy and the Wolverine, who did a two-pronged 'death attack'. That's when you bring death into the conversation and worst of all demonstrate a lack of fear and caring for both your own and other people's deaths. Wolverine began by telling us about how he visited the graves of murderers and even cannibals, buried nearby in the foothills, to scatter flowers on their graves. Lucy continued with the assault, recounting that, in fact, the Alpine Loop area was famous for a group of cannibal prospectors stranded during a snowstorm in a pass in the San Juans. Two out of five were eaten. The rest developed a taste for human flesh. When the blizzard passed the prospectors set out for the next mining town where they stayed six months. A string of disappearances coincided with their arrival, mostly children. The townsfolk finally caught on. A manhunt for the prospectors ensued. Soon after the suspects were taken into custody, they escaped only to be apprehended again and hanged. Sometimes the ghosts of the cannibals could be seen riding horseback through the forest and the mining towns at night. If they looked you in the eye, four days later you'd drop dead. The cannibals were buried near the Alpine Loop, that magical place Lucy had described as a perfect spot for a honeymoon.

And then it struck me. It was a sign. Camille and Diego Rivera. I told Ben we had to leave immediately. My nose stopped bleeding. I tossed the bloody napkin onto the table. "We've got to go find the graves of those cannibals."

Wolverine glared at me, wished us 'good luck' and lifted off his seat while Sabertooth slid out of the booth with his camcorder and grunted, following two paces behind his companion. Sabertooth stopped in the middle of the restaurant and aimed his camera at Wolverine, who did a cartwheel, then casually walked over and sat down at the counter as though nothing had happened.

We left the restaurant, bells jingling on the way out.

Once on the other side of the door, my symptoms vanished into thin air. I'd crossed a threshold – the world was brighter, my head was clear, my motor control was back. Perhaps the illness had in fact been a possession. Camille. She was trying to speak through me.

"Baby, the colour's come back into your cheeks."

"I feel much better."

"Well praise the Lord."

"That was strange, back there. Who do you think those guys were?"

"I don't know, pranksters or xenophobes."

Two houses down from the diner was a small, white clapboard house with the paint peeling off. It was set back from the road with a dog, silvery white, wolfish and lean, chained to a pole, pacing and panting amongst the usual collection of lawn ornaments – flamingos, pinwheels, birdbaths, gnomes, deer, and upon closer inspection, a disturbing trio of plastic sunflowers with faces like lawn jockeys. The dog was underfed, his ribs clearly visible. I could see patches of mange on his hindquarters and legs from where I stood. Benoît walked across the grass through the ornaments, toward the dog. The animal sat back on its haunches, panting and winking. Ben crouched down to let the dog get his scent, then stroked its silvery head. It was clear. We had to liberate the animal. Benoît unfastened the collar without a problem and put it on the ground. The dog looked up at him. Ben got up and made a motion to follow. The dog stood and walked at Ben's heel as we made our way back to the Montero. Ben opened the door and the dog jumped onto the back seat. He was some kind of dog whisperer.

We stopped further on to get dry and canned food for the dog and other sundries, then pulled over every couple of hours to let him out. It was as though he had always been Benoît's dog, he didn't stray and followed every command. In the car the dog lay on a piece of sheepskin on the back seat. I told him we were going to take care of him and protect him. He was one of us. There was something noble about him. We decided to call him Hemingway.

Ben took backroads through the fabled Red Rock Country on the Colorado Plateau, passing through orange dome-shaped marbled boulders, along rivers, under natural bridges and along slot canyons where giant rock formations stood like bands of Giacometti-esque hoodoos and goblins.

On the radio we heard that illegal raves in secluded, outdoor locations were happening all over the country. American and Confederate flags were being burnt as well as effigies of Uncle Sam and the President which were sprayed with gas-filled squirt guns, or else LSD, and set on fire. Some of the ravers were dying from dehydration and drug-related mishaps while half the causes of death remained a mystery. Ten thousand-odd people had been taken into custody. A guy phoned in to one of the stations and said it was the fulfilment of a Native American prophecy. A psychologist declared it a case of youth rebellion, with a set of behavioural traits that override class, culture, or race. At its heart it has to do with the struggle of identity to develop as an individual within society. Programmes and measures taken by society to end the risky, illegal behaviour, as seen at these raves, had thus far been, on the whole, ineffective.

Driving down backroads through the desert and the mountains, we came to a road through the San Juan

Mountains where it was as if we had been dropped into Switzerland with pieces of Americana populating the landscape. In lieu of medieval villages and immaculate cows with bells stood neon signs, diners, motels, and two pump, clapboard gas stations. Hemingway sat in the back seat, calm, on his haunches, eyes fixed out the window, his nose taking in the scents.

It was around nine in the morning when we hit the Alpine Loop. The pass was closed due to the snow. Still, we could see tiny details of the craggy peaks in the clear air, the rock turn from blue to yellow to tangerine and red. The moon hung in the pale blue sky – a frosted etching on glass. Snow flashed off the mountaintops in the sun. At the highest levels was tundra. We continued on rough dirt road that wound through ghost towns and abandoned silver mines, along vertiginous passes with vistas of lakes and rivers and the American Basin, a great valley which would be carpeted with wildflowers in the spring. Ben stopped the car and we got out to admire the view. With Hemingway, we walked far from the SUV, down into the dirt road until clouds began to roll in. The storm came so quickly and violently we knew we would be soaked by the time we reached the car. We all began to run. Then Benoît stopped.

He yelled over the din of the storm. "I forgot, I have two tabs of fucking LSD in my sock."

We stared at one another, breathing heavy in the torrential rain with Hemingway standing by. Ben reached into his sock and pulled the tiny pieces of paper out, tearing them apart and holding them in his thumbs as he pressed one to my lips and I opened my mouth. We both swallowed the tabs, then ran for the car.

It would be roughly forty-five minutes before the drugs took hold and would last at least six hours. There was no point in remaining there, cold and soaking wet, burning gas to keep warm and possibly running out of it. Back off the main road there must be a motel, it was our best bet. We began tripping before finding such a place but Benoît was serene. He said it was nothing compared to driving on ketamine. We came to a place called Sunshine Pass. The name was a beacon. A breadcrumb on the trail to finding Camille.

May 12th – 13th, Sunshine Pass environs, Colorado

When I awoke my mind was blank – a mental fog held me down in a wild, perplexing tangle. I felt as though I had travelled very far and struggled to remember who I was. My skin had the faint scent of burnt rubber. Something was dreadfully wrong. Nothing looked familiar. How had I come to be in this cabin? I saw the outline of another person in the bed and crawled slowly out of it, so as not to wake him. A dog that looked more like a malnourished wolf lay on a piece of sheepskin and raised its head as I passed by. Through the window moonlight poured over a picturesque woodland scene. I could see the stars.

After a while it became clear that I had awoken from an interminable and intense dream. I fixed my gaze on the beautiful boy with chiselled features and strong arms asleep in the bed. I remembered his name, and that he was mine – my Venus Acid Boy – and I was his wife, Eugenie. Hemingway. The dog was called Hemingway. In a flash it all came back.

We had rented a cabin surrounded by woodland – beyond which was a protected wilderness area – advertised at a rental agency in the nearest town, Black Hills, population two hundred and fifty-three, an old mining town perched on the side of a pass, hidden in the pines and rock. Main Street consisted of an old saloon, a Miners' Bank, a General Store, a bed and breakfast that had once been a whorehouse, a bakery, grocers and a hardware store. It was a Wild West shoot 'em up kind of town. The cannibals the waitress told us about were buried in a graveyard nearby.

The LSD was still acting on Ben and I upon our arrival, but Ben managed to keep it under control in front of the townspeople. I mostly stayed in the car with Hemingway, tripping off of the rainbows in his fur, the miracle of his being, the aliveness of the trees outside. Time was not constant and had a will of its own. Somehow, Ben collected and loaded enough supplies into the Montero to last a month or so as well as fly fishing equipment, hunting knives and a .22 rifle. The rifle was courtesy of the Miners' Bank for opening an account, and was the sole reason for opening it in the first place. We gave a false name. It was the only way to get a firearm in the vicinity with a minimum deposit of five hundred dollars. Bud Connors, our financial advisor for the transaction, explained with his left arm laid out on the table (his right gesturing every so often with his hand and seaweedy fingers so that his arm took on the appearance of a hydra-headed sea monster), that the firearm special had been on twenty-three years and running and was a matter of pride for the bank. When the owner was interviewed for PBS he declared they would have to pry the special from his cold dead hands before he stopped making it easier for people to exercise their constitutional rights. They even let us do a mock hold-up and take photographs with their Polaroid camera.

Mr Connors was a fan of horror movies. He got a far-off, perplexed look in his eyes which held the flintlock look of a cowboy and admitted that the moment he saw us come through the doors of the bank it was unsettling. He'd felt a déjà-vu that sent shivers down his spine. Connors told me I resembled a French actress in a horror film he'd recently seen. I was the spitting image of Lucy in Herzog's *Nosferatu the Vampyre* and with my dark eyes I also made him think of Snow White. The horror film, *Possession*, with Adjani, was one of his favourite films. Something in that pained and knowing look in his eyes confirmed he was no stranger to the complexities of the conflict between good and evil.

Then he spoke in a manner that was eerie and automatic, barely moving his lips, and said he hoped he wasn't being too forward when he suggested that I seemed to him to even resemble the actress in real life and spoke of the same quote Camille had once read to me, something the director, Truffaut, wrote in a letter to a friend during the filming of *Adéle H.* Camille had recited it so many times it had been burned to my memory: "You mention the pleasure I must have directing Isabelle A. It's the opposite of pleasure, it's daily suffering for me, and almost an agony for her. For her profession is her religion, and because of that our shoot is a trial for everyone. It would be too easy to say she is difficult, she is not. She is different from all the women in this profession and since she isn't even twenty, add to all this (to her genius, let's not be afraid of words), an unawareness of others and their vulnerability, which creates an unbelievable tension." Connors told me he could tell I took life very seriously.

This was no coincidence. It was a sign from Camille. Clearly she had possessed him. I felt her breath on my neck. She was here. We were in the right place.

Connors snapped back into his normal mode, as though nothing had happened. "That twenty-two is pretty good for hunting squirrels. Feels good to just pop their heads off. Things are cannibals, did you know that? I never did understand those folks, ooh-ing and awing over those God-forsaken creatures, taking pictures of them, feeding them nuts, or whatever." He half smiled and pushed a complimentary pack of bullets across the desk.

Ben asked whether it would be possible to get a firearm for bigger game.

"There's none of that this time of year, son. How long are you planning on staying with us, if you don't mind my asking?"

"Not that long."

"There's some of the best fishing in the country in these parts, I reckon."

"I suppose I'll be doing a lot of fishing then. Thank you for the recommendation."

We left the bank with our Polaroids, the gun and a new account book. As to the rental agreement, I remembered nothing. Ben must have carried me to the bed once we'd arrived at the cabin. The bedroom windows were open with white gauzy curtains fluttering in the breeze. It became apparent, all of a sudden, that I had been released from the charge. My head was clear, my body light and entirely my own without any other force coursing through it. Everything was more alive than I had remembered it; all that surrounded me took on a Biblical glow. The breeze carried in the scents of snow-capped peaks, pines, and dirt warmed in the sun with meadow grasses above it; all that mixed with the scent of us in the sheets, Hemingway's dog smell and the delicate scent of old wood furniture and the timber walls with the smoke of many fires burnt into them.

Sounds were amplified. A horsefly alighted on the top of the dresser, its landing making a dull thump in my ear which I could also feel as a vibration. Somewhere a timepiece ticked and although I could not see it I knew it was several rooms away, tucked into the top drawer of a dresser.

The phenomenon of this increase in awareness was familiar. Camille had called it 'jungle sensitivity' after reading a description of it in one of Colin Wilson's studies of the occult. Humans generally see ten to fifteen percent of the known colour spectrum and hear less than that of the acoustic. As a result of our studies and practices Camille and I entered into altered states where we gained perhaps double that in perception. Side effects included time shifts such as lapses and loss of short-term memory. It was during this period we began to demonstrate our uncanny ability to disappear into thin air and know all of a sudden where anything was, from the movements of Dr V to the location of a piece of our mother's jewellery hidden within the house. I had somehow attained the state again.

I lay in the bed next to Ben, concentrating on my breathing and keeping a level head, trying to adjust to the altered perception. At one point Camille and I had been able to capture the subtle electrical charges that emanate from animate as well as inanimate objects. The information contained in the charges coupled with our enhanced sense of scent, perhaps as good as a dog's, allowed us to detect the presence of fear, anger, disgust, happiness, surprise, arousal, et cetera, in all flora and fauna, as well as from inanimate objects such as rocks. Camille had said many times that rocks contained great knowledge. Their sense of time was much slower than ours, their knowledge more complete. Rivers, mountains, stars, plants, animals, all had a soul, all were intelligent spirits that could either help or harm humans. Like this we saw ourselves, among other things, as animists.

Dust particles caught the light around my Venus Acid Boy, asleep, breathing deeply beside me. I pressed myself up against him, feeling his warmth and the currents between us, kissing him all over to wake him up. He smelled like butter, maple syrup and bacon fat, and began to stir, his hands warm all over me. He had a dreamy grin on his face. "Terror," he whispered, as I got on top of him on all fours, kissing him from his chest to his groin.

We did it for hours, tenderly and like savages, until there was blood streaked across Ben's face and my arm, and on the sheets. We lay there, adrift. I traced a ship on Ben's back. "If you have a ship, and over time you replace the bow and the masts and hull and every board and even the steering wheel and every rope and every piece of it over time, is it still the same ship?"

"No, I don't think so. Not exactly."

I drew ships on his back with my fingertips until he drifted off to sleep, and must have fallen off myself. A murder of crows woke me, their calls shifting, cutting the air, and in a flash I was transported back to the woods in Maine, marching with Camille behind Dr V (sewn into a goat suit, deer antlers strapped to his head) carrying a burlap sack with our pet rabbits wriggling inside. We'd received them as a reward for successful remote viewing missions six months previously and had fallen in love with the creatures.

Dr V stopped in the centre of a circle of oaks, handed us a knife and said we had to slit the rabbits' throats. He would show us how to skin and roast them and then we would eat them if we didn't want to go hungry that night, or any other night, for that matter. We wouldn't eat until the rabbits had been eaten. His fantastical figure stood erect before us with the sacks of squirming rabbits in one hand, knife in the other.

After attempts to rouse us into action with the electrocuted dog collars and then out of frustration, slapping our faces with the back of his ringed hands, Dr V took the rabbits out of the sack and stabbed them to death in front of us. One generally thinks of rabbits as quiet, almost silent creatures but in situations of mortal danger this is not the case. Shrill, human screams came out of them, yodelling with blood, drawing murders of cawing crows that alighted on the branches until the entire circle of oak trees turned black and the air filled with their shrill, bitter calls. Camille picked the knife up off the forest floor and attempted to stab Dr V in the groin but he was too quick for her and grabbed her hand, pushing the blade down through her foot. She screamed and went for his throat while Dr V pulled the knife out, knowing Camille's character full well and that she would come after him. As it was, she ran toward him with a total disregard for her injury, picking up a tree branch like a club along the way, as Dr V fumbled and pressed on the dog collar control box, electrocuting her to no effect, while she beat him with the branch, jabbing it into his stomach to wind him, pummelling him on the head. He refused to go down, somehow took hold of the stick, and ordered us to go to our rooms.

Beside almost superhuman strength, Dr V had mental radar that seemed to know our exact co-ordinates at potentially any given time, depending on the clarity of the signal he was able to pick up. We sensed him, his eyes on us, like he was peering through a crystal ball, calling on his winged monkeys to fly and seek us out. The last time I had seen him he looked as good as dead – bloated and lifeless on the tiles after a killer bee attack. A year later, I began to feel the familiar, intermittent signals he'd used to track Camille and me when we'd strayed too far for too long. I reasoned that the sensations had been imprinted on me, that my problem was one of mental health, something like post-traumatic stress disorder, something that was wrong and had to be fixed. It was with a deep shock I learned he was alive and well from the woman at the records office – yes, he was still alive, he owned property. I heard corroborating eye-witness accounts. At first it seemed best to stay away, as far as possible, and continue to search for Camille. But then, on American soil, more and more, killing him properly struck me as the only option. I was going to go there and do it nice and clean, maybe with an icicle. We would have to wait till winter. That would give us time to prepare. No doubt he would see us coming. We had to rest and plan and get our minds clear. *We.* Benoît and me. A chill ran through me. I couldn't ask Ben to help me kill someone.

Ben's face hung over me. His eyes searched mine and found the horror that rose up around me like a swimming pool of blood. "Terror, you don't look so good. You look like you've seen a ghost."

"Yes, I have, I suppose."

He kissed me on the forehead. "Don't you know one of the reasons I love and admire you so much is for your courage? I know you've been through hell, baby. You're a survivor, made of strong stuff. From now on it's just you and me and I'm not going anywhere. I'm here to protect you to the death." He stroked my hair and kissed my lips. *"Je t'aime pour toujours et à la mort."*

More than anything in that moment, I wanted to kill someone. My heart burned ice cold with a rage and blood lust that threatened to suffocate me. I couldn't ruin Benoît's life and mine, end up separated, in jail. It had to be done cleanly and under the radar. I had to listen to Camille, to continue on the path we had taken as children. I had to invoke the spirits, appeal to them. If I could strike the Doctor down at a distance, this was the safest way. Of course, it was a longshot. I was never as strong in the arcane arts as Camille and depended heavily on her guidance.

Yet, I was not alone. It was clear she was here, in some form, making contact. Camille had led me to this place. I had to remember her instructions and follow them to the letter. I had to prepare. It was all that was left to me. Perhaps then I would see the man in the vision again, the one Camille and I called Deadeye.

December 24th, Passamaquoddy Bay Region, Maine

Maynard stopped reading. The woodstove ticked. Brigitte lay not far from him on a lawn chair cushion, eyes closed, her long-legged frame curled up like a sleeping fawn. The sky through the windows was blinding white and thick with cloud. Snow had just begun to fall. The radio said the storm would take several days to pass. He switched back to the police frequency, listening for anything that mentioned anything going on at the Vargas property.

Maynard did not know what to make of finding the backpack, the notebooks, the blood on the snow. Whatever it was, it was not a pretty picture. Clearly, something had happened. The Dr V mentioned in the account pointed to his neighbour Vargas. Whoever the author this Eugenie was it would seem that she had come for him, for Vargas, with good reason. He knew he was better suited to the task than Eugenie and her husband combined; one might even call him an expert. But he couldn't get involved, go up there, see what, if anything, was going on. It was a risk and it was not his place. Doomed enterprises cleave a life like a hatchet does a hand. Anything that got him involved any further in this business was not going to do him any good. He was supposed to be hiding out, not getting himself involved at the final hour in a long-term, ongoing vendetta that would surely end in more blood. Throwing himself as an unknown into the equation wasn't wise.

Maynard got up from the chair and went to a closet where he kept firearms and brought a Beretta FS92 with cleaning materials to the table in the centre of the room. Cleaning guns helped to cleanse the mind.

The backpack may or may not have been in Eugenie's possession at the time it was thrown, but it seemed a great probability that it was. There hadn't been anything else to determine the identity of the person who owned it. Five thousand dollars in cash were strewn about in billfolds with rubber bands around them between the notebooks. In the front pocket there had been some hairpins and a collection of small rocks, a quartz crystal, a matchbox with tiny semi-precious stones. All of this he had laid out on the table where he set down his Beretta.

Maynard recalled hearing the name Eugenie mentioned once in his life, a long time ago, in the papers – a missing heiress. There was a two-million-dollar reward. Did Eugenie have a twin sister? He thought hard, summoning up any information he could remember on the case, anything he'd read in newspapers or heard on the radio or in conversation. He would have been on his second tour of duty. The story was familiar. He'd wanted to find whoever kidnapped the girls and rescue them, like everyone else, until the futility caught up with him and they all but disappeared from his mind.

In his youth many such furies were born and died within him in the face of tragedy and injustice. He'd felt like he would devour the sun and turn it in on itself. It was a struggle not to cross the line during his years of service. He'd come close to disaster a couple of times, but somehow, with a great force of will had avoided it and even won medals. Being in the sniper division had given him many chances to prove himself and he did so with impeccability. He broke records in all areas of the field – infiltration, field craft, special reconnaissance, surveillance, target acquisition, et cetera. His brothers-in-arms were often spooked by his mental and physical accuracy.

Maynard sat with the contents of the backpack in front of him on the table, pulled back the hammer of the Beretta and cleaned in between the crevices with a small piece of cloth sprayed with a new gun cleaner, then used a small wooden rod with the cloth to clean the barrel.

The man referred to as Dr V in the notebooks had a residence in Maine, which was where Maynard sat, presently, on a parcel of land abutting a property belonging to a Dr Vargas. Was this coincidence, or were the men one and the same? Had his neighbour held the heiress and her sister captive for all those years? He was beginning to distrust his sanity. He had come to the cabin to lay low until he was given the all clear. The last time it had been only several months. He had looked forward to extracting himself from the general population and the complications, as well as heartache, it inevitably brought. His working relationships were beginning to affect his mental health. Getting back to the basics with nothing to do but fish and *hunt with Brigitte was going to set him in a clear direction, whatever that may be. There wasn't anything else he had to do, until he found the backpack. Maynard took the spring and guide rod apart and cleaned them. The woodstove whined; logs fell inside.*

No, his mind was playing tricks on him, making too much out of very little. He had to remain sober, logical, immaculate. If not, he would surely go over the edge. Even Brigitte had been giving him doubtful looks as he circled the table contemplating the contents of the backpack. However, hypothetically, if Eugenie was the missing heiress, what would that mean? There was mention of a father. She was going to see her father in California with her husband, a reunion that had been indefinitely postponed by the unforeseen events at the casino. It fit, but was hardly definitive. The girl in the notebooks sounded about the right age. The heiress may very well have been hiding in Europe. Had she been found? It was possible. In all those years it was conceivable she had been found and he had not heard about it, but doubtful as it would have made headlines. Or would it?

If he intervened he would be an unknown factor in their plans; his presence might set them off guard. Who knows how they would react? It was best not to get mixed up in it at all. Yet, in all fairness, he was already involved. There were the journals and the five thousand in cash. What of that? He had already decided he would hide them in a place the law would never find to gain more time to think it through. Maynard picked up the barrel and wiped down the outside, then took a long tear of cloth sprayed with gun cleaner and attached one end to the top of the chair ladder, slid the cloth through the barrel and made the string tight so he could scrape the insides. Why was he thinking of his mother?

Maynard grew up mostly alone, the only child of a widow who had taken to drink and consoling herself in the arms of military men who could never replace her dead husband. She lived to please them and was shaken every time she looked at her son, the spitting image of his father who had died when the child was an infant. From a young age he had been left to his own devices and ran wild with packs of other boys, yet even in their company, for the most part, he felt alone. During this time he thought of his father every day without fail – the impressions he drew of the man changing with time. He had photographs and had learned bits and pieces from his mother when he pressed her. Maynard's paternal grandfather had described his father to him – kind, handsome, didn't need much discipline, drawn to army trucks and toy soldiers from the time he could crawl. He loved the great outdoors. His grandfather and father had gone hunting and fishing from the time Maynard's father was a small boy. He had also been a good hunter, a good shot. Maynard found out little else in addition to this. His grandfather's time on this earth was interrupted by fatal lung cancer.

There was a box of photographs that had belonged to his father with photos from when he was in Vietnam and of his boyhood in Alaska where he had a dog as white as the driven snow. When Maynard asked his grandfather what had become of the dog he learned she was shot by someone on the outskirts of town who took her for a wolf. He imagined his father's grief at the loss of his companion and suspected there were many things like this in his father's life he would never know. Maynard went through the snapshots time and time again, memorizing his father's expressions, his stance, his world, contemplating who he was as a man.

He also had an address book that had belonged to his father. When Maynard was seventeen he decided to call one of the numbers, a Don Grady. Grady answered. Maynard introduced himself and asked whether he had known his father. He had. They were stationed together for a year in the Mekong Delta. He told Maynard his father had been a courageous man, dedicated to serving his country. He had never faltered – he was a good man and a good friend through and through. There was none better to trust one's life with. He assured Maynard by telling the young man he knew he must be strong because his father had been. He said he should be very proud of him. Maynard thanked Mr Grady and decided that was all he needed to know, all he could know. There was no need to call anyone else. Maynard would live up to that. He would become a good man who served his country.

In high school, he divided his time between studying in his room, the town library and the playing fields, running, training, preparing his mind and body for the demands the military was going to put on him. He left his mother to her abstractions, seeing her seldom. She was mostly a ghost to him, haunting the northeast bedroom on the second floor with her liquor and later pills from the doctor. Maynard had a part-time job at a gas station and slipped an envelope with cash under her door every month. He knew she would probably spend it on liquor, but she was a grown woman and could make her own decisions. He wanted her to know he was still there and that he wasn't judging her. She was presently in a nursing home with dementia after her third husband shot himself in their house. Maynard had found her emaciated and raving mad in appalling living conditions, no running water and the house infested with mice. She was barely alive. He brought her to the hospital and when she was well enough, arranged for her care in a specialized home to which he sent money every month.

There was a storm coming. Better to go now, rather than later, if he was going to see what was happening at the Vargas estate. It could be the last opportunity he had before it became foolish. No – he had already decided; he wasn't going to leave the cabin. He wasn't going anywhere. He was going to make something to eat. Then hide the backpack and its contents. Maybe he would read the rest of the journals. And then he would sleep. He could spend long hours sleeping through the storm. The night before he had experienced something that was near to a revelation – he recognized he was dreaming in the dream and at that moment everything became very real, as though it were reality, perhaps even more so. Yes, he remembered, the colour and definition had also been more vivid. He'd thought that he was so alive and so awake and full of energy that when he awoke he would be exhausted from all of the activity, but found that it was the opposite – the sleep had thoroughly refreshed him. He hoped it would happen again that night.

Maynard went about making dinner. It was going to be potatoes, beans, and squash with venison, a staple. He found he didn't need to eat very much in a day. He gave the deer he killed to a butcher who also had a smokehouse and in return got smoked venison, fresh venison, beef, chicken, whatever he wanted the man could get. He and Brigitte had a varied diet. They were living high on the hog. As it was, there were enough supplies to last a couple of weeks. The main roads would be cleared almost overnight once the storm broke, but the small ones would take longer. This was why he had a plough on the front of his truck.

After he ate, he let Brigitte lick his plate and then fed her. Maynard added wood to the fire in the fireplace, sat beside it and continued to read. Once he had read them all he would put everything back in the backpack and secure it in a hiding place.

May 14th, Sunshine Pass environs, Colorado

In the woods behind the cabin I found plants similar to ones Camille and I had used called Cochise's Paint, only the small, yellow pods had red powder inside rather than gold. I would use them to make protective symbols on our bodies for the ceremony. Camille and I had often used Icelandic magical staves from The Huld Manuscript – a compilation of Icelandic magical symbols, sigils and charms carried down from the time of the Norsemen which had served Camille and I well, although the sleeping spells and the killing rune had had no effect on Dr V, which was not to dismiss them. He was a formidable opponent, versed in the black arts before we had even been conceived.

Western psychology seeks to chart the psyche without taking into consideration that it is but one province on a more extensive map. About a year after the kidnapping, Camille began to explain things like this to me – knowledge she had gathered from books in the libraries of the house where we were held captive. She explained that Bön practitioners and other ancient, shamanic civilizations across the globe had made great steps in charting these territories unknown to psychiatry, and had left clues to reaching them. We then began a concerted effort to search through all the anthropological material, folklore, scientific and religious texts we could get our hands on, sifting through the pages, looking for correlations, composing hypotheses, taking notes. I acted as her assistant.

To venture into these lands was treacherous – spirits and supernatural beings bent on mayhem populated the hills and dales. Camille once explained that ultimately, the universe was predatory (there is always a chain – a top and a bottom, spiralling into eternity). It was a predator of extreme beauty, like the jaguar, beguiling and wise – a carrier of great power and knowledge far beyond a human's capacity to know. Camille and I could not comprehend it, but we stood to gain access to intelligence that made our hearts beat faster.

Camille was drawn to ancient, subversive religions which worshipped a primordial cosmic energy with a divine female, creative, and procreative power that was responsible for every act of creation and change. It was the force of cosmic existence, of ultimate liberation. We followed clues in our texts to tantric possession – a state reached by magical incantations and rituals in which humans are transformed into divine beings with supernatural powers. Like this we held a chance of defeating Dr V. It would not be easy as he carried a formidable bag of black magic, while we carried hope, determination, and rage.

Camille and I encountered the demonic in these supernatural lands. Our childhood was rife with their possession. We were snatched out of our bodies as we knelt to perform enchantments, often failing to recognise our energetic limits. Dr V was forever plying us with pills and practicing exorcisms. The ones that did not possess us acted like poltergeists, hurling china and crystal goblets across the dining room, knocking chairs over, switching the lights on and off, producing objects out of thin air. Still, we kept on. Camille and I knew we had to bleed, to endure unspeakable hardships, to prove ourselves worthy of the knowledge. We persevered with the hope that one day we would triumph. I had faith that the spirits and divinities would most certainly be able to terminate Dr V and find Camille and took heart in the fact that I wasn't embarking on a completely implausible affair.

There are many ways to reach these places which lay outside the realm of 'everyday reality'. One such passageway is the portal of the dream, but it is no ordinary dreaming. When one becomes aware that one is dreaming, this is the first step. Most people have had the experience. I remember when it happened to me I got a jolt. I felt liberated with the truth, the realisation that I was, in fact, not awake but in another world which looked and felt and even smelled just as real, perhaps even more so.

Camille and I employed many methods, the oldest known, such as those of the Bön and Buddhist teachings, of the ancient tribes and civilizations across North and South America, the Hindus and the Jains. All ways offered diverse techniques to enter these worlds through the dream and navigate within them. We wore strings around our index fingers during the day to remind ourselves to become lucid when we went to sleep each night. Later we wore gold rings. We meditated, practised breathing exercises, and performed rituals to the deities.

Once one is able to sustain lucidity in the dream the next trick is to gaze at everything, not focusing on any object in particular, in order to get a hold on the world. Resting too much attention on one thing causes the surroundings to dissolve at first, and ultimately hurls one back into wakefulness and 'everyday' reality. As one gains more experience the landscape may be seen in more intricate detail. With practice and the proper guidance come greater control and the discovery of new abilities. Information is revealed, epiphanies are reached. One exercises more influence in the dreaming world. The adept dreamer recalls everything, eventually.

Ceremonies, meditation, breathing exercises, certain plants and herbs, near death experiences, and even sound could bring one to these worlds (or altered states, as psychologists refer to them).

In all instances, ceasing the internal dialogue held the key. The incessant narrative in our heads traps us in the collective reality we are so familiar with, shrouding all other realities like a fog. When the mind is empty of thought and highly tuned to a state of high concentration, other means of perception are revealed. Reason's grip falls away, as it does in dreams and the hypnagogic state, and in pours something akin to intuition. Like this, one navigates with one's personal power, or will, which is ultimately much more accurate than logic. It is this potentiality that we sought.

As the journey is perilous certain rules must be observed. For example, protective symbols must be worn. Sticks and rattles can also be used to drive away the malefic spirits. Camille had once told me that Lamaist magicians and sorcerers could subdue and tame the demonical beings to use for their own purposes, but this practice was no less evil than the beings themselves, and could negatively impact our rebirth and our ability to attain enlightenment, so was best avoided.

I felt closer to Camille in the forest. The signal was clear, far from the psychic and electrical interference of the cities. I continued in a south-westerly direction under the pines, collecting things – blue jay, crow, cardinal feathers, most of them along my way, almost as though the wind had carried them to me, as well as tiny pebbles to fashion rattles out of stick, twine and egg carton, and any rock or stick that felt it would be right for my practices.

Hemingway and I came to a place where we wound between boulders until we met a brook and followed it along its banks, crossing over where a great pine had fallen. I also collected tree branches along the way that most resembled stakes so that I could carve messages to the deities and post them in the ground around the house. I hoped I'd catch the familiar scent of sage. The sweetgrass had already been found in a meadow. Sage purifies and drives away evil spirits while sweetgrass attracts the benevolent ones. I tried to remember anything at all Camille had told me in regards to the herbs and the specific deities they called, which signs to make, which songs to sing.

Eventually we found sagebrush. I took enough to make two eight-inch smudging bundles. I noted I was adapting well to this new way of seeing, to the 'jungle sensitivity', no doubt because Camille and I had experienced it before. At times it was as though the nervous system of every living thing was connected to my own. I was gaining in personal power and had to do everything not to let it slip from my possession. It was part of the honing mechanism I would need to find Camille.

Back at the cabin, Ben was still sleeping. Hemingway followed me into the bathroom and lay on a rug at the door, standing guard, as I took a bath with lavender oil, burning sage and sweetgrass in seashell ashtrays to purify myself, with the intention of emptying my mind of thought. Once out of the bath I rubbed myself in oils and put on a gauzy pale peach and violet slip with flowers of various sizes scattered all over it. My reflection in the full-length mirror gave the impression of my naked body floating in water, covered in blossoms like John Everett Millais' *Ophelia*.

In the living room, weathered timber eaves came to an apex at the top of the ceiling. The walls and floor were made of wood. A mounted deer head hung on the south-facing wall while paintings of hunting and nature scenes were rampant. Above the great fieldstone fireplace, a framed, five-foot trout trophy had been mounted. I made a small fire, throwing sage and sweetgrass onto it, fanning the smoke all over the room with feathers, then addressing the deities of the four directions with burning branches of sage. I then went about constructing an altar on a coffee table in the middle of the room.

In the end, all of the elements were represented: a mound of earth, a bowl of water, lit candles, a crystal shaped like a pyramid, a piece of wood with the names of Shinto spirits carved into it, a turquoise polar bear amulet, the blue jay, cardinal and crow feathers, a hummingbird nest, wildflowers, a rock, et cetera. I moved the furniture and drew a circle of chalk on the floorboards, then set about cutting out a round paper doll made to look like one of the Bön deities, the Queen of the World. I painted one eye and made a wish. When my wish had been granted I would paint the other eye. I made food offerings, then constructed rattles and feather earrings out of fishhooks. Sage and sweetgrass continued to burn. On the altar I lit mounds of the powdered incense Camille had made which I carried with me in a jar on my travels. It was a mixture to evoke the goddess Asherah, the Queen of Heaven. Thick, white smoke spooled from the red-hot mound that glowed and spit tiny orange sparks. I repeated an invocation Camille had taught me as I sat within the circle of chalk in front of the shrine and settled in for a long meditation.

At the first light of dawn Ben emerged from the bedroom with a cigarette in his hand out of the ceremonial smoke to find me engaged in prayer. "Baby, it's time for the ceremony." My tone was soft, yet serious, and surprised me because it was new and sounded like 'me', yet did not. I went to him and raised myself up on the balls of my feet to kiss his cheek.

"Terror, what have you done to the living room? Looks like voodoo or something?"

"It's the oldest spiritual tradition of Tibet, for all intents and purposes. This is how we're going to evade capture and find Camille."

"I need *un café, ma chérie.*"

"It has to be done when the sun's rising. I'm going to purify you with the sage and then, here," I held up the crow feather earring, "you need to wear this." The night's vigil had left me feeling as though I could not be contained, shining and brilliant, drunk on the wonder of creation.

"No, baby, my ears aren't pierced. I can't wear that thing."

"The sun's rising already. We can do it right now."

"What are you saying?"

"It's easy with a hot needle. That's how Camille and I did ours. You have to suffer for the spirits to take pity on you. You have to bleed. Then they're more likely to come."

"No, *mon coeur*, no ritualistic sacrifice before *le café*. It's sacred to a Frenchman."

We compromised to save time and he had a coffee whilst I pierced his ear in the kitchen. Benoît did not flinch. I pricked my finger and pressed it to his earlobe and like that joined our blood and tasted it. I had done it before even thinking about it and didn't mention it to Ben, or know if he noticed, for fear he would think it was crazy.

"*Allez, mon bébé*. When's this ceremony going to begin? I'm hungry." Benoît sat back in the chair and took a drag off his cigarette. I prepared the red powder with water until it was a paste and painted both of us with protective symbols, explaining all the while how Ben was to empty his head of thought and find his spirit animal, which was the purpose of the ceremony.

I bathed both of us in sage and sweetgrass smoke, then drew kohl around our eyes. We moved to the former living room, now a temple, and sat in front of the altar within the circle of chalk where more sage, sweetgrass, and incense burned. Ben sat cross-legged on the carpet edge with the drum and found a rhythm. I shook rattles, danced and chanted, trying to empty my mind of thought, and finding it difficult.

After a while I decided to try another way in – the rope visualization. For this I had to concentrate on creating a rope with the imagination and grab hold of it. This act breaks the membrane between everyday reality and the dream world, enabling one to step into the dream territory completely aware that one is dreaming and embark on the next steps to gaining more understanding, power, and knowledge of that world. One might enter and exit these realms, as Camille and I had, through a bright light, or a fog – other times it happened instantly, clear as day. The shift was immediately apparent, the quality of everything changed with each component of reality more complex, luminescent, with a greater richness of colour, sight, and sound, and comprehension.

With practice Camille and I were able to have more control over the events and the places we visited in these dreaming worlds. She began to know things about the past and the future that unnerved everyone around us. At times I became so lucid in my dreaming it was almost as consistent as this reality, but I was far behind Camille. I travelled to mountaintop villages reminiscent of Tibet, to jungles, through cities, along plains and in grottos on horseback, sometimes journeying by canoe, or magic carpet, all the while asking people I found questions about existence or the nature of the universe. Most often they answered in gibberish. Part of the problem was that the characters I was meeting weren't as lucid as I was. I eventually trained myself to become so comprehensible I could string my sentences together clearly and coherently and ask answerable questions whereas the people I met were not to my level and speaking nonsense. When I wasn't lucid enough in a dream, I fumbled around in a daze and spoke the same gobbledygook.

Camille did not have these problems. She described valleys carpeted with wildflowers, green snow-capped mountains, forests and Shinto temples where she conversed with supernatural beings. She said they were helping her to cultivate a 'heightened openness' – the most intimate form of knowledge would be revealed to her when she was able to 'capture the mood and vitality of things', to become so attuned to everything in the natural world, to the spirit, that she knew the heart-mind of a thing. She meditated on the transient nature of the world and the melancholy beauty in the life of cherry blossom petals. Whereas, I kept hoping I would find someone in the dreams who actually knew something.

I continued to chant and dance within the circle of chalk and shake the rattle, while Ben drummed and I turned to all four directions, visualizing the rope. Time and time again, my hand passed through it like a phantom. A strange dizzy lift, or sensation of swimming precipitated me into a world of stillness. Suddenly I knew I had grabbed hold and was enveloped by a dense fog. There were presences all around me – feathers touching my skin, furry paws at my neck – though I saw nothing. I began to sing a song to my power animal. There was the scent of deer on the wind. My faculties told me there were trees, rocks, birds and other creatures, as well as a gurgling brook. Time was irrelevant. In the end, I found myself back, dancing around the altar. Ben stopped drumming. I gave a few last shakes of the rattle. There remained something undefinably astir in the cabin.

"I feel energized. Is this how you do it, Terror? Make witchy rituals in the morning? Are you a witch?" He got up, came to me, lifted me up, spun me around and set me down again.

"Did you experience anything paranormal?"

"No, I didn't see any ghouls or spirit power animals."

"Any angels? Did you feel anything at all?"

"Baby, you're my angel." He kissed me on the forehead. "Look at you."

Hemingway circled around us, then disappeared to paw at the porch door to be let out. I kissed Ben on the chest and darted for the door where Hem was waiting impatiently, eyes fixed straight ahead in intense concentration, as though he could see through the barrier, which, in a way, he could, as he was no doubt seeing with his sense of smell. He took off like a shot when the door opened, circled around the back of the house and dashed off into the forest.

I descended the few steps to the wild lawn and scanned for a level area where I could practise gymnastics floor exercise passes. Before me was a river, thrashing and bubbling like a cauldron, rushing toward the south-east. All around was woodland. I found a good place in the grass to stretch and went through the splits and bridges, getting up to do forward and back walkovers, and then side aerials. I could still do a standing back flip. After that, I did a series of round-off back handsprings with a layout flip. The last trick I'd learned was a double full, on the spring floor exercise. This consisted of a layout flip with the body rotating seven hundred and twenty degrees before landing in one spot as if plucked out of the air by some unseen hand. I wasn't sure I was going to attempt that move on the grass, but after several passes of layouts with three hundred and sixty degree spins I had confidence I could do it. I ran and landed the move perfectly, about four yards from the tree line and had turned toward it when all of a sudden a hum like gigantic insect wings thumping the air set the hairs at the back of my neck on end, then vanished, followed by chiming like a crystal glass being rubbed, permeating everything, changing octaves. I noticed Ben was behind me. "Did you hear that?"

"I don't hear anything." He pulled me close to him. "I came for you, Terror." An all-consuming blood lust filled his eyes. He picked me up and wolfishly bit and kissed my lips as he carried me wrapped around him into the wood. We made love up against a pine tree and ended up on the floor in the leaves and needles and dirt, scratched, dazed, and bruised.

May 14th, Sunshine Pass environs, Colorado

Brooding on existential ideas is really a bitch. I don't think the general population ponders the question too much. We're alive and we just do things and occupy ourselves without thinking about our eventual downfall.

I got out of the existential thinking naturally with time, but it always came back. I remember how remarkable it was when it first disappeared. I spent a few months brooding on it after my big psychosis that put me in hospital in Switzerland, but then it faded and I returned to relatively normal thinking.

Camille often brought up death and the afterlife in conversations but she knew that it was a taboo subject, something sacred, so we began to speak in code and only had in-depth conversations about it at our secret cabin in the Maine woods. Sometimes it was almost as if Camille looked forward to dying. It excited her, like an adventure. Other times she would be left deeply troubled in contemplation of it.

The unearthly hum that came and went through the woods and set my hairs on end the day before troubled me. It was a song – the haunting call that moths produce. Camille used to say that if you could hear this particular call, clearly and cleanly, and if you were impeccable, immaculate of heart, then it would remain with you for the rest of your life. I had heard the sound before, with Camille.

Ben stood on the riverbank casting his line. I was submerged up to my waist in the river, half-naked in my underwear with a bow I'd fashioned out of juniper and squirrel gut from the squirrels Benoît shot. He had hung their insides to dry near the fire and knew about these things, getting the elasticity just right. He also taught me to make arrows, as well as trout tickling – the art of rubbing the underbellies of the fish with the fingertips, mimicking the river grasses so that the trout falls into a momentary state of trance and can be lifted up and tossed onto land. Ben had picked the skill up one summer working on a farm. The old man who had taught him was also an expert in poaching pheasants and educated Ben in that art as well. They went to the local public house with three others before heading out to appropriate the game. The old man ordered beer for everyone as well as a cognac. They toasted and then the old man took a handful of raisins out of his pocket and dropped them into the cognac. The men drank and talked and smoked. When the beer had been drunk the old man tossed the glass of cognac back, put the raisins in his pocket and said it was time to head out. The party walked out of the village and into the forest that belonged to a tobacco magnate. The old man tossed the raisins as though he were planting seeds then made a gesture and said they would all go back to the bar. The men drank another round of beer after which they returned to the spot where the raisins had been thrown. A dozen pheasants lay on their backs, unable to move, ready to be collected and their necks broken. Benoît had many stories like these.

Hemingway stayed close by at first as Ben and I fished. I don't think he'd ever seen a river before our coming to the cabin. He pranced along the bank, giddy and anxious, pouncing and splashing the surface with his paw, baffled by what we were doing in there chasing after the trout until he finally bounded in punch-drunk and scattered them. It was beautiful to watch, his grace, his moments of discovery and freedom.

We were fortunate to have landed in such an idyllic spot with a river so close by and I derived an unearthly pleasure in swimming, propelling myself down, deeper into the cool underworld – the realm of the naiads. Once, on a trip to Germany with Dr V, Camille and I stayed at a retreat beside a river in the forest. We were convinced naiads lived in the stream – we had heard them singing – and decided to go looking for them. Camille and I conspired along the way to win them over so that they would transform us, and take us with them. We would never have to see Dr V again.

We shed our clothes at the riverbank and swam downstream listening for the naiads with water lilies in our hair, swimming for hours in the blue, pearly light of the gibbous moon overhead, which lit up the woodland scene, giving the surface of the water a blue-green glow. At one point we stopped and rested above water, as silent as we could be, and listened and felt all that was around us. We both turned our heads simultaneously and saw the outline of a deer, then dipped back underwater to explore and continue to look for the water spirits.

When the light of dawn came through into our subaquatic world our skin took on a yellowish green glow. I watched Camille twirl, her hair wild, dark and dramatic against the pallor of her skin as she moved her legs and gestured with pearls of bubbles streaming from her outstretched arms, calling to the naiads. It was then, with the light, after all of her spirals and incantations, that Camille and I were really able to explore, chasing one another through corridors of rock and slimy fronds of vegetation, past tangles of lily pad stems where tadpoles congregated in phalanxes. We rarely came up for breath. It seemed a sign that we were transforming, that the naiads beckoned. As the sun grew higher we knew we were running out of time, and could not be sure any metamorphosis had occurred. We hadn't seen any sign of the naiads, so we went running back through the forest to get into bed before our absence was noticed.

Camille had told me that the Olmec believed rivers and lakes were portals to other worlds where the supernatural beings lived. They performed ceremonies to honour them at the banks and like this entered hypnagogic states and the dream realm. For Camille and me these places were also sacred entrances to other worlds. We even believed the water to have an intelligence. I felt Camille's presence, there in the river. I had stepped deeper into the world Camille and I had begun to explore.

Camille taught me that man has, in fact, seven senses. Telepathy, or the 'telepathic sense', is highly developed in barbarians and savages, while it remains atrophied in most civilized persons from continued disuse. Wild animals also possess the faculty which acts to protect them from predators and to locate prey. Jaguars, especially, are known for their ability to predict what their prey will do next with astonishing accuracy. Then there is the 'clairvoyant sense', which allows for remote viewing – the ability to travel with the mind backwards and forwards through time to any location in the universe. It is with this sense Camille thought the saints contacted the angels, the Native Americans spoke with their dead ancestors, the Norse communicated with their gods and goddesses, et cetera. It can also be accessed through dreams. Needless to say, we felt we'd gone deeper into magic, into the shamanic realm where everything is alive, everything has a consciousness constantly sending and receiving waves, currents and vibrations. Everything is energy which can be seen when one acquires the vision to see it with.

The heightened awareness came and went. I wasn't able to control it. When it passed it left me with a mental confusion not unlike a time in Rustler's Valley, South Africa, when three Swiss girls gave me a 'potion' in a field of poppies and told me it was mostly liquid ecstasy. The drink made me groggy so I went to bed while they disappeared, giggling, into the starry night. I dreamt I was a wildflower in the valley meadows that encircled the cabins. It was not an ordinary dream – it was of the kind that seems absolutely real, completely lived and authentic and even more vibrant, or more real, if that is possible. My human consciousness dissolved, time compressed and I spent an entire lifetime as the flower. When I woke I couldn't shake it. The flower lingered, at odds with the complexity and brutality of the human's existence. I sat dazed and mute in the back of the Swiss girls' van for days while they took turns driving, waiting for the two consciousnesses to come to terms with one another. I'm not sure that the flower ever rubbed off and disappeared completely. I don't think I was the same after that.

Added to this confused mental state – preceded by an intake of LSD, snake venom, whatever they gave me in the hospital, as well as quinine and laudanum – I could not help thinking of the possibility we were wanted in Nevada. The weight was so great I could not sustain it for long and let it vanish before it became an unhealthy obsession. How long would they look for us before they gave up? Ben hadn't said anything; he didn't seem worried. I had to trust that Camille had led us here, to safety, and that we were on the right path. I was doing all that I could to protect the area, there were ancient Norse talismans staked into the ground in the shape of a pentagram, and I was practising the daily rituals each morning and evening at the altar in the living room without fail.

I watched Ben, waist deep in the stream, casting the line, lassoing it up into the air. In that moment I knew that losing him would be worse than anything I could imagine. It felt dangerous to love that much. A world without him would surely destroy me. I had to believe we would find one another, no matter what – after death, in future lives, just like I had to believe I would find Camille.

Benoît caught four trout, fat and dazzling with rainbow scales and specks of silver. I had speared one and quickly cut its head off. We laid the fish out on a rock slab near the stream. I said a few words for their safe passage back to the world of the spirits. Benoît taught me how to gut them.

"Do you think we should eat the guts?"

"Hell no, Terror. The crows will eat them."

"Yes, we can make offerings to the crows." I went to get tobacco, sweet grass and sage to burn them at the rock slab with the fish guts. Crows were messengers between the gods, guides, carriers of spiritual law. I appealed to them by the riverside while Ben fired up the grill. Afterward I went inside to prepare the fish, rubbing ours with oil, lemon and ground black pepper and leaving two plain for Hemingway. I set them on a plate and carried them out to the grill where Benoît was stoking the coals. "What I could really use is some hashish."

"I think it's all pretty much weed in this country."

"Mmm. Well – well yeah, that could also be good."

"I have a secret to tell you, but not now."

"What's the secret, Terror?"

"Mmm." I put my finger to my chin and cocked my head, my eyes locked on his. In my wandering for the ritualistic paraphernalia I had picked up the scent of cannabis. I was going to tell Benoît immediately, but was caught by a mischievous cupidity and held back.

"Terror –" Ben grabbed me, lifting me up giggling into the air then spun me around until everything was a blur and finally set me back on my feet where I collapsed, dizzy and slightly nauseated. "That's what we do to naughty girls who keep secrets." I looked up at him with big eyes. "Aww, Terror." He picked me up, removed fragments of leaves from my hair and pulled me in close to him with my head cradled in his arms, my cheek against his chest and kissed me on the top of the head. I rubbed my face into him and got his scent, then took a knife and bounded off into the forest, pulled by a force I had little control over. Hemingway followed me through the bracken, over fallen trees, between boulders and beams of light illuminating hordes of gnats, transformed in the sun, their tiny, translucent, golden forms almost sparkling, giving the impression of beings from the fairy realms.

I was charged, on fire, unable to stop myself from leaping up into the air to diffuse the energy. Volts ripped through my palms. The forest writhed, hissed, sparkled and hummed all around us. I listened for the voices of the spirits and bid them to come, to show me the way and to protect us. I came upon a dead badger. It was an omen. Hemingway had led me to it.

Camille once told me the future could be seen in the reflection of badger's blood. She had learned this from her readings on Native North American tribes. It was auspicious to find the animal. The surface of the blood is to be looked upon like a mirror where the future can be seen. Hemingway sniffed at the corpse. I called him away and told him to sit, then went closer to examine the dead animal. Flies scattered. The eye had been punctured and the throat slit. Clearly a fight. I had to find a receptacle to contain the blood so that I could gaze at the blood. Nothing in my immediate surroundings offered anything I could use. I began to run, heading back for the house to get a teacup, with Hemingway outpacing me by the length of his body. We flew over the bracken, side by side, gaining speed, zigzagging through the wood with my reality shifting around me, between the 'everyday' and the 'jungle sensitivity'.

Ben's voice came from far off with a tinny quality. "Baby, get over here –" Hemingway went off like a shot, leaving me behind. Once into the clearing that surrounded the house Ben caught sight of us and made a motion for me to come to him. I ran onto the grassy area and did a pass I had done in one of my gymnastics floor routines which began with a front aerial and ended with a backward full twisting flip in the air, spinning like an ice skater, then bounded over to him.

He kissed me on the lips. "You're my little ninja."

I wanted him. I wanted to slip out of my clothes and for him to take me out into the woods again. I threw him a smouldering look, turned in my hot pants and stood in front of him, pulling at his shirt, lifting it up and running my fingertips over his stomach, up to his chest, kissing him, nipping at his lip.

"Terror. You're a sex pest. I'm going to give it to you good up against one of those pines, but now I'm grilling fish. You were gone forever. It's almost done." He shot me a wolfish grin.

"I've just come back to get a teacup."

"A tea party with the woodland creatures?"

"Yes, something like that. I'll be right back."

"I hope so because dinner is almost served."

Teacup in hand, I darted off with Hemingway back into the forest to the spot where he had found the badger. I made a cut with a Swiss army knife under its foreleg and held the animal upside down with the cup in the other hand, collecting perhaps seven tablespoons of blood. It was enough. I knew where I would bury the badger.

Earlier I had found Hemingway inside a thicket of wild rose bushes which made a domed roof where below the forest floor was carpeted with forget-me-nots, pink and white and cornflower blue. The scene, with beams and threads of light streaming through the rose bush ceiling, was enchantment. I brought the badger there, buried him and said a prayer, then gazed at the surface of the blood in the teacup. I saw the man from our visions and guessed it meant I would soon meet him.

Mosquitoes began to appear in larger numbers. It was the hour when they all come out, like the witching hour or the hour of the wolf. Hemingway and I ran back to the cabin. I found Ben in the kitchen with dinner served. He was smoking a cigarette. "Good timing, *ma chérie*."

I sat down across from him at the table made of wood with a Formica top, looking very much like something that had been there since the late Forties. "So, what did you get up to this time? With the sprites and water nymphs and such?"

"I'm not sure you want to know."

"C'mon, tell me."

"We found a dead badger and looked for the future in its blood."

"I see." He took a bit of his food, chewed and swallowed.

"And then we buried it in a field of forget-me-nots."

"Did you see the future, in the blood?"

"I'm not sure. I saw a man I'd seen as a child, in visions. I've mentioned him before. I know this must all sound crazy."

"No, Terror, crazy doesn't even come close." He grinned and squinted one eye.

We ate and the fish was good. The beans had been sautéed in butter and garlic until some of them were burnt and it was delicious that way. Benoît ate quickly, his head bent over his plate.

Camille believed it took seven years to get every trace of a man out of your system as all cells in the body regenerate during that time. Her attitude toward male and female relations was largely based on a study which found that men emit chemicals during lovemaking capable of imprinting themselves into the women's cells. Women, however, do not possess anything like this power men have over them. The presence of an attractive woman can raise a man's adrenaline levels and cloud his judgment, but is not as potent as what the man could ultimately do to the woman. Camille reasoned that falling in love was a loser's game for the female sex. "The man will always have more power over you in the end if he has chemicals, like a magic potion that infects and intoxicates you, ultimately attaching itself onto your very DNA."

At the time I thought I was in love with James Dean and couldn't even fathom what it would have been like to get infected by his man chemicals. My amorous, contrary talk frustrated Camille no end (after all he was dead) but she was no better because she was in love with Robin Hood. We were children then and did not yet know that the ways of romantic love were more complex than chemicals. Crossing paths with Benoît had confirmed this. What a long journey it had been, and yet, everything felt as though it was just beginning.

After lunch we set up tin can targets in the woods and practised with the rifle. Ben had experience with firearms. When he left his last foster family he signed up for the army (from which he was discharged for insubordination). "First you godda get a good grip. Hold it, just here," Ben stood behind me, guiding my arms. "Hold it firm until your hand starts to tremble. Then release and relax." He taught me the stance and then about the sights, how to zero in on the target and how the sight alignment was more important than the sight picture. You had to be very calm and know how to hold your breath, breathing easy in and out with the target in your sights, then waiting till the natural respiratory pause for the squeeze like shooting clowns at a funfair. Ben said some gunmen were so good they could shoot between heartbeats.

Then we made love up against a birch. I told Ben my secret – that I'd smelled cannabis in the air and guessed it was about seven miles away. He was sceptical but said we might as well go looking for it in the morning.

May 17th, Sunshine Pass environs, Colorado

Upon finishing breakfast Ben announced we would go after the cannabis. He lit a cigarette and I cleared up and prepared provisions for the journey while he filled a backpack with anything we might need in an emergency. It was to be the longest expedition we'd taken since our arrival.

Mist hung and moved like ghosts around the girths of the young Ponderosa pines, thick as telephone poles, pricking the sky, dwarfing us. Hemingway had the air of a wolf in his wild element. He bounded ahead and circled us, catching up only to adventure off again. At one point the forest gave way to a meadow with grass up to my knees, where wild irises also grew, as well as Queen Anne's lace, buttercups, and daisies. Hemingway cavorted through the field with his hind legs moving like a jackrabbit. Benoît recorded birdcalls with his Dictaphone. "I'm gonna use all these sounds in my next production and call it 'My American Honeymoon'."

"Baby, you're so romantic."

"You got any idea how far away the weed is?"

"I can't be sure but about a couple of miles."

Hemingway ran ahead of us and disappeared.

"The best place to find your power animal is in the forest."

Ben smiled with a glint in his eye, mocking me. "Is that so?"

"It's serious. You have to want to, with all your heart and soul and we have to fast. It's not to be taken lightly."

"I'm game, baby. You teach me and we'll go find our animals."

We walked further on. Hemingway appeared in the distance through the pines, circling, barking, pacing back and forth. I skipped off, ahead of Ben recording a murder of crows, to see what Hemingway had found.

The structure looked worthy of an archaeological dig. The careful way the stones were placed made it look like the entrance to an underground tomb. I threw a rock in and counted seconds as it dropped into darkness. It hit dirt maybe seventy feet down. I lay out in front of the opening and stuck my head in. A metallic buzzing sound purred in my ears, changing scales like a musical tone to produce an eerie rhythm that made my skull and teeth hum and held me fixed until I fell into an altered state.

On several occasions, Camille and I had sighted a creature in the Maine woods, which emitted the same noise. Because of its enormous, red, mesmerising eyes, I have only one several-second film clip of it in my memory banks – a giant moth-like creature maybe seven feet tall, levitating up and down in Earth's easy gravity emitting a whirring, singing sound. One moment the Mothman was there, the next gone.

Benoît crouched down next to me.

"There's something down there."

"It looks like a well."

"Put your head down there and tell me what you hear."

Ben lay down in the dirt next to me and stuck his head in. "Well, I'll be damned." He took out his Dictaphone, pressed record, then stuck the device down the well. "*Mortelle.*" He jumped to his feet. "I can't wait to get back to France and put all these sounds through my sampler." I sat on the ground and stared up at him. "Chop-chop, baby, we've got to find that weed."

We walked further on, crossed a stream and came to a grove of quaking aspen. A woodpecker swooped past us, flew close to the ground then shot up into the nearest tree. I noted that in Indo-European mythology the woodpecker was a prophetic bird with magical powers – the bird of fire and lightning. It was a good sign. I told Ben but he wasn't listening.

"My God it's gonna be good to smoke. Can you tell what kind it is, from the smell of it?"

"I don't know, Hindu Kush, Blueberry, something citrusy, something that smells like candy."

"Really? I know something that smells like candy."

A surge went through me. Ben backed me firmly up against the nearest aspen and lifted my dress off. We ended up in the dirt. Afterward I saw fresh scratches. We sat there taking deep breaths like divers coming up for air.

We walked. Hemingway kept disappearing and coming back.

"We should teach Hemingway how to find weed."

"Why? I can do it."

We eventually came to a section of the forest with mammoth Ponderosas – in between these giants, in the distance, stood a lone, whitewashed, dilapidated church with parts of the roof missing and vegetation growing through it. We approached cautiously.

"Holy Mary, mother of Jesus. Is that – what I think it is?"

This was the place. We approached the building and went inside. The intoxicating perfume of at least thirteen different strains of cannabis hit us as we stood among the trembling plants, most of them towering above us. We made our way through the nave, down what appeared to be a small path in the centre with coloured light from the stained glass windows falling on the leaves and the heads of the crystallized buds. The chancel was still intact. We stepped up onto it. There was an antique-looking, rustic table and chairs made of carved oak. On top of it was an array of pipes, most of them glass, a couple of the Sherlock Holmes variety, and a corncob. Four tumbler glasses and three ashtrays with spliffs crushed out were arranged haphazardly about the table.

The altar was still there with Christ's paint mostly flaked off behind the podium.

"Nice set-up."

In the sacristy stood a cast iron stove, a brass bed and a desk. It didn't look like anyone did much writing there. Not a scrap of paper to be seen, or even a pen. No notebooks, but there were a few books and magazines. We decided not to trespass too long and walked back out through the cannabis foliage.

Once outside we noticed what looked like a break in the trees and went toward it, eventually coming to a meadow on a hillside. Past the tops of the trees below, the San Juan Mountains snaked out in front of us with their peaks forming the horizon. In the centre, rising out of all the green, was a mountain with a rock face shaped like a Mayan pyramid, the colour of ochre sandstone. We sat down in the tall grass and wildflowers. Ben lit a cigarette and leaned back. I made a chain of buttercups, tied it into a circle and put it on my head like a crown. Hemingway was nowhere to be seen. We ate sandwiches and drank tea.

"Baby, I can't believe our luck. A cannabis plantation. Our neighbour's got a cannabis plantation. I wanna meet this dude."

It wasn't long before the owner came. Hemingway had made friends with his bitch, a large lilac pit with a white chest. The cultivator was a bull of a man over six feet tall in a wife beater, with a fine-featured face, yet still very masculine, and with dark curls underneath a trucker's cap, coon tail hanging off it. He carried a shotgun. It looked like a pump-action Remington. "Y'all don't look like no undercover agents."

"No, in fact, we're outlaws." Ben stood up to greet the man.

The cultivator looked at Benoît sideways. "Well, I suppose it matters what type of outlaws."

"We had a couple of big wins in some casinos in Vegas, then one of them gave us trouble when we wanted to cash in and one thing led to another."

"I see. Well, I'm kind of prone to skating above the law myself." He played with a toothpick in his mouth. "Stupid to step right in it though." He turned to me. "What's your name, darlin'?"

"Genie."

He grinned and then squared Ben in the face. "My brother, you're a lucky man."

Ben's face hardened. "Yeah. She's a Terror, like a genie in a bottle. She's my wife. I'm Ben, and you?"

"Travis. Well, congratulations. You two make a very fine couple. Let's smoke to that, to your union and to many adventures and happy times and fortune and fame and all of that crap. I've been with the same woman for thirteen years now – got seven girls and a boy." He made a motion toward the church. "Wanna see my ladies?"

"Most definitely."

Travis looked over his shoulder at Ben. "That is, if you haven't already. I can smell it on you so don't lie."

We followed him down the path and entered through the weatherbeaten church doors.

"Me and a friend of mine planted these seeds after a trip to California. We had read in *High Times* that it was the place to go for seeds, so we went. Travelled around collecting seeds and horticultural info, then came back. It was the summer after our high school graduation. A long time ago now." He pointed to a bush that had been pruned into a mushroom shape, yielding much larger, more compact buds. "We've developed our own strains, of course."

We walked up the wooden steps and sat down at the table at the far end of the chancel to the left of the altar.

"Which one, princess?" Travis motioned toward the pipe collection. I chose the corncob.

"No, no, we can't smoke out of that. It's too rough."

"I've never smoked out of a corncob pipe before."

"Look, here, we'll smoke a glass one." Travis chose a small, discreet blue and gold zebra-striped glass blown pipe and loaded it. "So, where're y'all from?"

"I'm French."

"I'm American, originally."

"From where?"

"All over."

"I swear I saw your face somewhere."

"People are always telling me I look like some actress. I'm not famous."

Travis passed me the pipe. "Yeah, it's best living life under the radar." He winked at me, then looked sideways at Ben. "You hit the jackpot there, bro. All of the cherries."

"She's not on the auction block," Ben squared his eyes with Travis's, "so don't be speaking about her with any disrespect."

"I never meant any, brother." Travis turned to me. "My apologies if I offended you in any way, young lady."

"You're forgiven." I gave a half-hearted smile, not fully understanding what had just happened between them. It seemed that Ben didn't want anyone speaking about me in the third person while I was still in the room, or else it was the jackpot and the allusion to money. Perhaps it was all of it and also something men sense in-between one another. I lit the pipe and took a small hit and could tell from the cool, tingly smoke stream that the weed was some kind of super-bred, turbocharged variety. Needless to say I saw stars and little tweeting birds circling my head and felt as though I had taken a right hook to the chin. The shit was strong.

"You alright, baby? Come here." Ben motioned to me. Somehow I found my way to his lap and lay my head on his shoulder with my arm resting across his chest.

"She's as white as a sheet. Packs a wallop, don't it?"

Benoît took a hit and exhaled, holding tight onto me. "Good shit. Tops. This weed is as good as Amsterdam."

"You know, when I first saw your animal, coming through the trees at my bitch, I thought I'd seen a wolf and I just said, my Lord am I going to be having half wild pups? Beautiful animal."

"Yeah, we rescued him. We've only had him not more than a week."

"What're you doing to get rid of that mange?"

"Lemon juice."

"Yeah, that's not bad." Travis played with a toothpick in his mouth. "Do you want to come back to my place? Meet the woman and children?"

"Well, I dunno –"

"It's not so far – it's down near the river." Travis pointed east.

Ben stroked my hair and asked me if I felt like going. I raised my head up, sitting there perched on his leg, then looked into his eyes and nodded in the affirmative with a "Sure" to seal the deal. I got to my feet first then walked down through the corridor of cannabis with the two behind me until we exited the church and Travis took the lead. Instead of going east as I had thought he indicated before, we travelled west, into the sun. Benoît and Travis discussed marijuana farming and the ills of the world. Travis reckoned that the legalization of hemp would save America. He had copies of the plans for automobile engines that ran on water and air someone had given him from the Internet. It was proof of the wrong-doings of the government. Something had to be done before it was too late.

Travis called for revolution. Like the French had done in 1789. The Kings of Oil had to be taken down. Everyone had to grow hemp. This was the solution. Benoît agreed. It sounded very sensible, except that the French Revolution brought the Reign of Terror and then Napoleon the First. There wasn't any guarantee something equally awful wouldn't happen in the United States.

"Well, the French didn't have weed in their equation."

"Nor did they have handguns."

"I see you've got it all figured out."

"I'm not stupid enough to think I've got anything figured out."

Travis smiled and touched his temple. "I never pegged you for stupid, brother. If there's anything I've learned, it's to be on your guard. Always have your wits about you, exercise the mind. Be flexible. We can always be better. Personally, I read history books to relax."

"I could really drink a beer right now."

"Soon. Have patience. It'll be worth it."

We walked through the Ponderosas and then through pines. The dogs followed, frolicking and panting, zigzagging ahead then looping back to walk alongside us, only to go off again. Travis explained his rewilding program for an ideal America, which would take place after the revolution and the collapse, something he was hell-bent on bringing about. In a nutshell, all mankind would return to a wilder, natural state but with the knowledge we have today. Yes, many people would die during the transition, but it was a sacrifice, for greater freedom. The true liberty the American people had been promised was nothing but a false idol. Travis looked back at us and winked. "Rome did not actually fall – it was transformed."

Travis's house was an ode to a Southern Gothic horror novel with its Victorian mansion constitution, slate mansard roofs and Russian cupola. Set back fifty yards or so from the edge of an overhang where below stood the remnants of a ghost town, it stood like a mirage.

"This was the banker's house, back in the eighteen-hundreds. Nothing's changed since the time of the Pharaohs. The slave state lives on. Only the oppressors are nomadic, they travel the globe, making it much more difficult to pin them down. My grandfather bought this land for a song in the Forties. Now it belongs to me."

We walked up over the hill. His children came into sight. Travis took the toothpick out of his mouth. Four girls between the ages of perhaps eight and sixteen were in the midst of a game of croquet in front of the house while two others, not more than three or four, sat under an enormous oak with a rope swing hanging from its boughs, one child playing with dolls and a tea set, the other with a train under his arm. Upon sensing our approach, the four older girls stopped the game and turned in our direction, mallets in hand, eyes fixed on us. Time slowed down. I was possessed by a strong sensation of déjà vu. Ben took my hand and kissed the backs of my fingers as we walked, then let go. It was as though I was catching a glimpse of the master reel, the hand of fate. A robin flew across our path. Travis spit on the ground. We stood in front of the honey-haired band, barefoot, in summer dresses, and were introduced. The eldest, Electra, brought her hand to her necklace that spelled out her name in gold cursive and gazed at me with her dark eyelashes and the ardent eyes of a cat charmed by a snake or an insect. "Girls, this is Genie and Ben." We all said hello. "Where's Scarlet?"

Juliet answered. "She's napping."

"And your mother?"

"Baking a cake with the baby."

"C'mon." Travis motioned for us to proceed to the porch. Before we turned and left the croquet party for the house Electra and I caught one another's eye. I thought I saw the mark of recognition. The girls went back to their game.

Travis told us to have a seat on a wicker sofa and disappeared into the house with the shotgun. The dogs stayed on the front lawn, investigating the scents of all that had passed there. I distinctly felt Camille's presence. The wind sibilated through the trees. I watched as the girls congregated at the end of the double diamond of wickets, their voices warbled by the wind. They were deciding whether or not to play the poison version of the game. Electra tossed the mallet to the side and went to the small children who were fighting over a teapot.

Travis came through the screen door carrying a six pack of bottled beer.

"Nice place you got here." Ben took the drink from Travis with a nod and popped the top off with a lighter.

"Thank you, brother. This is my piece of the American Dream. Doesn't get much better than this." Travis sat down next to us, whacked the beer cap off with the table edge and passed the bottle to me.

"Seems like an odd place to have a town, out in the middle of nowhere."

"Well, the river's just over there. Maybe you can see it through the trees. But, yeah, it *was* off the beaten path. This was one of the Johnsons' places, famed gangsters of the times. Supposedly some crazy shit went down here. We used to come here as kids." Travis sat deep in the creaking wicker armchair, his eyes slits like a reptile's, focused in on Ben.

"You and your wife?"

"No, not her. Rachel's not from around here. I found her, in the woods, wandering around in a t-shirt and underwear. My friends down at the police station have been looking for a clue to her identity for eight years. She was speaking some strange language when I found her." He took a sip of beer. "People disappear here. People disappear everywhere. They gotta end up somewhere."

"Delicious beer – thanks for the hospitality." I raised my bottle to him.

"Yeah, none of that watered down crap. Real beer. Real weed. Real nice view."

Benoît looked square at Travis and nodded.

"So, you two just passin' through?"

"Yeah, it's our honeymoon. Then we don't know what we'll do. Maybe go back to France."

"Yeah. France. Say, in your country, they don't let off nuclear explosions in the deserts out there do they? And not tell anyone about it."

"I don't know. They probably do, somewhere, in some desert in Africa or something. They blow a lot of shit up over there."

"Yeah, you're right. They probably all do it. That's why, well, let me tell you something, just before Rachel showed up I used to go camping out in the desert. One time I was off-roading, far away from anything, then all of a sudden there was this, I kid you not, mushroom cloud, far off in the distance and one hell of a shockwave. I mean, I was nowhere brother, nowhere. I turned that vehicle around on two wheels and raised dust out of there. I got sick. Doctor said it was radiation poisoning. I lived though, obviously. Then I did some research. Because this was weighing on me, you know?

"So. Operation Trinity. Nineteen-forty-five, the first test atomic bomb is let off in New Mexico, in a place called the Jornada del Muerto desert. Then there was this one in the Nevada desert called Operation Tumbler Snapper and Operation Hardtack II. Hardtack I was in the Pacific, the Bikini Atoll, Enewetak Atoll, and Johnston Island. Of course there were hundreds of servicemen who died terrible deaths from all the radiation poisoning. Bastards just don't learn. They even wanted to explode a nuclear bomb on the moon, let it go off like the Fourth of July, to scare the Russians. How something like that could even be considered is, quite frankly, some real fucked-up shit.

"My friend telephoned just the other day and told me he saw on his local news that a nuclear reactive rod, the kind they use in hydraulic fracturing, you know for the natural gas? It just fell off a truck and got lost. Everyone's to be on the lookout for it. These people can't keep getting away with this kind of crap. In the end, that gas ain't natural or safe. Don't even get me started on that fracking bullshit. No amount of money from suing their asses is going to replace our resources, the water we drink. It's a lose-lose situation. Those bastards need to be exterminated." Travis was resolute.

"I dunno. I never heard about any of that."

"Well, the point is, they're still doing it, my brother, right now. And what I've just told you is the tip of the iceberg. Do you know what cleans radiation from the air? Hemp. That's right. If I could I would plant a forest of it around here. When all is said and done, living in the woods, we're freer up here.

"Sure, we're not going to take the system down because it's just too powerful. But we're not gonna make it easy for them are we? We're gonna give 'em hell. Like the fucking raccoons." He flashed a brief, sly smile our way and then became serious. "I once saw a coon take down a pack of dogs, slit their throats and claw their intestines out all over the river bank. That coon killed every last one of them before making it to the river's edge and succumbing to its wounds. There was tissue and pieces of guts, eyeballs and fur all over the place like it'd been sprayed out with a hose. Hell of a fight." He leaned forward and pointed. "Happened just down there, past the town, through the trees. I buried the dogs, then that coon I buried somewhere else because I don't know, it just didn't seem right to bury them all together. They were enemies."

"Makes sense." Ben squinted his eyes and gave a slight nod.

"Life is strange, brother. What was that Doors tune?" He began to sing, "People are strange..." then stopped after a few lines and nodded. "I think this is a good place for children to grow up, don't you?"

"It sure is picturesque."

"You two planning on having any kids? If you don't mind my asking –"

"We hadn't thought about it."

"Well, you should. It's good to have children. Especially people like you. We got to have children and teach them. Make a tradition. Rome wasn't built in a day. My grandmother's living with us. My mother died a few years ago in a car accident. Father died a long time ago. But Mammy's still here. She's eighty-seven. She's just working on some quilt in there. She loves to quilt. She's like a nun, quilting, reading the Bible. She was a bit of a wild child in her time. She's got a mild case of dementia and can't hear in one ear. But she can get around okay with a walker." Travis picked up his baseball cap with the coon tail hanging off of it and put it back down.

"It sure is peaceful."

"No one bothers us up here. It's better than living in town, or a city. You can hunt, fish, do just about anything.

Grow a shitload of weed. Supply the towns and power everything with solar panels."

"Sounds pretty good."

"I even built a sauna, down near the river."

"Yeah, sounds like paradise."

"Pretty damn near close." Travis raised his beer bottle and drank.

The three of us sat without speaking, admiring the view. The dogs crisscrossed back and forth through the croquet game and then went off, out of our field of vision.

"Well, I don't mind if your dog impregnates mine. I'm not going to worry about it." Travis twisted a toothpick in his mouth.

"Yeah. I hope we're going to be able to keep him."

"What do you mean?"

"Well, we're going to need to leave the country. We *did* commit a couple of crimes back there." Benoît took a sip of beer and then a drag off his cigarette and blew smoke rings.

"We might be going to Peru."

Travis looked absentmindedly at me then turned to Ben. "Where? Back there in Nevada? What'd you do *exactly*?"

"Well, Eugenie here is a genius for cards. No limit Texas Hold 'Em especially. She taught me how to play and made the plan of attack. We took down a couple of casinos for maybe sixty grand. The last one didn't want to pay up so we took security as hostages, got the money, drove off."

"Damn, brother." Travis adjusted himself in the chair. "You might just be the kind of people I've been looking for. This could be destiny calling at our doors."

"How so?"

"Well, we'll see."

"We'll see what?"

"If you've got what it takes. If your story's the real spit then I would say that you do, but is your mindset, your *morality*, is *that* in the right place?"

"I'm not a rebel without a conscience. But I'm not planning on sticking around either."

"Brother, a man can get lost in these woods. Your identity can just get wiped off the map." Travis offered us more beer and flipped the caps off with a lighter and passed them to us, then served himself. "What do you all say to civil disobedience in the face of a political and corporate monster that's devouring our children and our land, our sanity, the gift that is God's green earth? What do you say to a brotherhood that fights together for the good of society at large?"

"I'd say it's complicated." Benoît sat back further in his chair and took a drag off his cigarette. "I've heard what those ravers are doing out there in the desert, burning flags, effigies, dying. We were even at one of the gatherings, in the desert. I dunno, man, what were you thinking?"

"Is that so? I hadn't heard about that. I've just come back from nearly a week out there," Travis pointed toward the forest, "where I can think," then sipped his beer and sat back.

"It's been on the radio. We came across some candy ravers and followed them to a rave. They were burning effigies, maybe doing some witchy rituals. Then we got shot with LSD from a water gun and don't remember too much. Genie got bit by a viper. Ended up in the hospital."

"Jesus." Travis scratched his forehead.

"I can't imagine where this all is going to lead to." Ben flicked cigarette ash into a nearby ashtray and a blue veil of smoke passed across his face. "I think for us, it's best we leave the country."

"Those ravers. Good on them. We got some coons loose out there. Wasn't what I had in mind, but civil disobedience is good. People setting fires, that's a good distraction, just need to keep it going until the opportunity strikes." Travis turned to me and looked me coolly in the eyes. "Did you say you got bitten by a viper, little girl?"

"Yeah. In the Mojave. I'm okay now though. I've got a high resistance to poison."

"That so." Travis gestured to Ben. "Well, she's immune to poison, so what superpower do you have, brother?"

"I have very good reflexes."

"Show me something then."

"I dunno." Ben scratched the back of his neck.

"Well, let's just go down there and we see who can knock who out first."

Ben stubbed his cigarette out. "Okay."

Benoît followed Travis's hulking form onto the grass maybe thirty metres from the edge of the girls' croquet game. I sat at the top step of the veranda.

"Alright. Any time, bro." Travis assumed a fighting position. Ben grabbed Travis's wrist with his right hand and pulled it, jerking Travis forward as he back-fisted him with the left. Travis went down with a thud.

I ran down the steps. "Ben, why did you have to go and do that?" I knelt to the ground next to Travis, down for the count.

"Sorry, baby. But anyway, there's no harm done."

Electra came over and kneeled next to me. "Daddy?"

Travis opened his eyes. "I'm fine, Lectra. Your father just met his match." He propped himself up on one arm. "Well done, brother. You're quick. Son of a gun." Travis got to his feet. Electra had one last look at her father, turned and skipped back to the game.

Travis put his arm around Ben. "Let's smoke to that. Shit, bro, you might just have some of the quickest guns in the west. Wouldn't want to go against you in a shoot-out. What's your experience with firearms?"

"I was in the army in France for a couple of years."

"I thought as much." Travis patted Ben on the back and made a move back to the porch. Ben followed.

I stood at the top step. "Don't you think you should put some ice on that?"

"Naw, darlin'. It's not that bad."

We resumed our positions on the porch. Travis packed a pipe with a marijuana bud he pulled out of his pocket and handed the smoking device to Ben.

"Thanks, man." Ben lifted the pipe up in salute to its maker, lit it, inhaled and exhaled a cottony white cloud of smoke that broke and tumbled in waves past my face. I wasn't going to hazard another go and passed the pipe to Travis.

"I like you people. Too bad you have to go so soon. We could have caused some real trouble. I've got big plans."

"I think we've gotten ourselves into enough trouble already." Ben took a sip of beer and grinned. "And to make matters worse, we put our money in the local bank. It was the only way to get a firearm. It fucks things up even more. I don't think we'd come down from the LSD yet. I just had to have that firearm they advertised in the bank window. I remember some octopus in there. I vaguely remember communing with some sea creature." Ben rubbed his head. "We shoulda been gone today already. So, we're just a little reckless is all. If those bills are marked, and the Feds get involved, well –"

"Jesus, brother – that was stupid. They usually do have numbers on those bills. I can only do so much but I'm tight with the sheriff. He's one of my brothers-in-arms. Part of this weed operation is his. We started it together. He can tell me if anything like that's on their radar. But his reach is obviously limited. Anyway, he doesn't want those Feds up here probably as bad as you."

"Don't you think they would have found us by now if they were looking? The money's been in the bank for a week or so." Ben sat deep in his chair, un-rattled.

"Who knows? I'd head out latest within the next six, seven days if I were you. Keep moving."

With the danger out in the open like that, it gathered more reality and more weight. Was it paranoia to think that we were being hunted down? That the serial numbers on the bills would be reported? Were we not safe here, at least for the time being? How much longer did we have? I had to find Camille. I had to investigate the well. Her presence was here; I could feel it.

Electra bounded up the steps, light and easy, and sat down on the floor in front of me, legs bent under her, a clump of forget-me-nots in her hand. "I've seen a girl who looks like you. She lives in a well around here, at least that's how it was in the dream. Her name's Camille. I wrote a story about her."

I became hyperaware of everything around me; blood ran to my cheeks.

"I've seen that story. Electra, you've got talent. Don't ever give that up."

My heart beat in my ears. Camille was near. It *was* the well. Camille and the vision of the Mothman at the well. She must have been abducted by the creature and brought here, to his lair. "My sister's named Camille. I'm trying to find her. Do these dreams tell you anything more?"

"She said she was waiting for someone. She was sad. She couldn't stay long. I've tried to follow her, many times, through the woods, but she always disappears into the well."

I told Electra she'd helped me more than she knew and Ben announced we had to head out, get back to the cabin so we could organise ourselves and formulate a plan.

"I could help you, brother, what do you need? Stay for dinner. You can meet the wife. Get some home cooking. See the rest of the operation."

Ben said we would come in the next few days, if that was amenable to him. Travis went and got us a CB radio and set it to his channel. "Get me on this, brother, if you need me."

"Thanks." They bumped fists and Ben called Hemingway, who came running from around the corner of the house.

We said our goodbyes, Travis handed Benoît a bag of weed and Electra made a gift of a bottle of homemade lemon vinegar insect repellent, insisting she spray all of us before we headed off. We were glad she had when the air thickened with swarms of mosquitoes; it seemed to help. When we came to the well we didn't stop. It was imprudent to say anything to Ben about the Mothman, or Camille being down the well. He wouldn't understand. I would return at night when he was asleep. We saw another woodpecker.

May 18th – 24th, Sunshine Pass environs, Colorado

Ben smoked enough weed that evening to place himself firmly within a cannabis coma. I left the cabin with Hemingway, a backpack full of equipment and a kerosene lantern. I was too high-strung to access my newly acquired 'jungle sensitivity'. Despite my best efforts, I couldn't suppress the elation that spooled up inside of me at the prospect of making further contact with Camille. Electra said Camille lived in the well. All of the signs had led me here. It had to be true.

The night was clear, the stars magnificent, multi-coloured, glittering from the dark vault above. It was cold, but not enough to discourage the mosquitoes. I wore Electra's repellent and had also rubbed citronella and lavender all over myself and sprayed Hemingway. Moths came for the flame of my lantern and made shadows that magnified their dimensions on the forest floor. With the light and the moon almost full, the forest appeared as a silver gelatin photograph. Owls called and other night creatures made noise from the trees and undergrowth. The air was crisp and fragrant. I remembered there were mountain lions in these parts. Camille had said that big cats can read minds and that the jaguars were the best mind readers. I prayed we would not cross paths with one. The lantern would help to frighten any predators we might come across in the forest.

After an indeterminate amount of time, we came to a wooden hut with a mud roof covered in peltry laid out to dry. I thought I saw beaver, rabbit, mink, perhaps badger. Maybe even skunk. Smoke came from a chimney. As we approached ever closer a dog appeared from around the side of the abode and stood facing us, teeth gnashed, shaking with the reverberations of its growling. The hairs of both dogs stood on end. Hemingway wrinkled his muzzle and bared his teeth, returning the dog's warning with a low, menacing snarl.

A man appeared with a shotgun from out of the shadows behind the dog. I half expected it to be the man in Camille's and my visions, but when the figure came into the light of my lantern I saw it was not him. This man was much older, unkempt and unwashed, and smelled of carrion and dog, sweat and urine. His whole being exuded animal ill-temper and menace. "Looks like you've lost your way, little lady." His voice was honeyed and deep and he spoke with a slight drawl.

"I'm sorry to trouble you. I was looking for an old, disused well."

"It's not recommended to walk around alone in these parts at night. Especially for a woman so fine as yourself."

"Yes."

"I'd just go back home and look for it in the morning, if I were you."

"I'll follow your advice."

"Which way did you come from?"

"The river."

"Well, just keep going that a way," he gestured behind me to the east.

"Yes, I will. Thank you, kind sir." I bowed my head.

He tipped his hat. Hemingway and I turned around and passed along the side of the hut in the direction the man had indicated. Beaver paws hung on logs and the carcass of a deer dangled from the side of the primitive dwelling. There were more pelts drying outside the door as well as animal bones. It looked like the den of a wild animal. The thought occurred to me that he was, in fact, one of the dead cannibals who had escaped hanging and hidden in the woods – not a man at all but a spectre condemned to haunting the foothills.

We came to the well almost as though we had fallen upon it. Down on my hands and knees, perched at the edge of the abyss, I heard nothing but the groaning of the wind and was struck by a fear that gnawed at my insides. Was I being paranoid, or was it my intuition? Hemingway stood beside me until I got up and began tying a rope to the lantern so that I could lower it down. He began pacing back and forth in a semi-circle around the well, head cocked to either side each time he paused. The shadow and light upon the stones made the shaft into the earth look reptilian.

The rope was far too short. I couldn't even see the bottom. My plans to investigate had come to naught. Yet again I had acted foolishly, this time by going out into the wilderness at night with my heightened sense of awareness on the fritz thinking I would shimmy down into the black unknown of a well I suspected held Camille captive.

There had been many failures, due to my stupidity and lack of foresight. At times I'd contemplated finding our father and asking him for help. The thought filled me with elation and dread. The truth was that I barely knew him, and he had never come to save us. Camille and I had given up on him long ago. I could not go to him – that was all. He would undoubtedly ask what had happened and I could not tell him. And then, it would be the end. The end of everything I had been so passionately constructing. Either way, if I told him, or if I said nothing, he would begin to imagine that something unspeakable had happened. I didn't know which was worse, the recounting of the actual horror, or the one he would have constructed in his mind. He was better off without me and the pain I would eventually deliver him.

Hemingway began to whine and point and soon after we heard coyotes. It was time to move out. Yet another failed mission; my heart sank. I was losing my grip on reality. I could see the madness coming, as bleak and frenzied as a plague of locusts. The darkness beyond the lantern light fell like a screen onto which my mind projected celestial beings that turned into demons and Mothmen creatures, complete with blood-curdling sound effects. Then, who was to say it wasn't the real thing? At this point, I couldn't be certain. Were we being followed? Was it the cannibal prospector? I had looked into his eyes. Lucy, the waitress, had said that once that happens, after three days you drop dead. The fields of my inner compass had gone haywire – mania descended on me like a bolt of lightning. I thought of mountain lions and a thousand other things, my mind racing from one tangent to the next while repeating an ancient Norse spell for invisibility, running at a pace that felt more like flying, manoeuvring the lantern in such a way that it also flew but didn't extinguish. I came to the conclusion the real danger wasn't the mountain lion. It was the two-legged ones, with their intellect, creativity, opposable thumbs and menace; they were the ones who posed the greatest threat.

The clearing surrounding the cabin came into view; the din in my head stopped. I was relieved to set sight on the cabin. Benoît was sleeping soundly. I slipped into bed next to him and gently kissed his chest until he pulled me close and on top of him. The charge began. I wanted to set fires. I wanted Ben to consume me. We got so close I felt I had slipped into his psyche – I saw him through countless lives, bodies, forms, bursts of light.

"Jesus, baby. What a way to wake up."

"Isn't marriage wonderful?"

"Hell, yes." Ben passed me the glass of water beside the bed, then took it back and drank before he picked up a spliff from the ashtray and lit it.

I turned on my stomach and studied his face in the blue smoke. "I saw your spirit animal, baby."

"We need a plan."

"Maybe we should go to Peru."

"I was thinking France. Take the money we have and invest it in something. I keep going with my DJing.

Maybe we could open a club, something illegal tucked in somewhere."

"Even so, by the end of this we are going to need a bigger bankroll for something like that. We could always go to Canada."

Ben sat down next to me and stroked my hair. "Jesus, I'm stupid. We never should have crossed back over Nevada state lines. You wouldn't have gotten bit by that viper, or got dosed with LSD." He passed me a spliff, kissed me on the cheek and pressed my hand again. "I'm sorry, baby."

"You didn't mean for it to happen. It must have been too charged with possibility not to."

"Jesus, you say the damnedest things."

Dr V had money. Camille and I had seen stacks of bills in metal boxes under the floorboards and I had taken a hundred thousand with me. At the time, it seemed foolish to take more. There were also safes in the house but those would require an expert locksmith. A few hundred grand would be enough. There might even be more hidden in other places. I wondered whether I had the courage to return. I got out of bed, looked at myself naked in the mirror and turned to Ben. "Tiger, do you want some scrambled eggs and toast?" I'd learned how to bake bread in the old gas oven and was proud of my toast.

"Mmm, yes, kitty cat." He got up, pulled on his jeans and wandered into the living room where he would open a window, start a fire and smoke a spliff or a cigarette until I brought him coffee.

In the kitchen I picked up a frying pan to put it to heat and noticed a figure etched into the centre of it. Where many American households have seen the face of Jesus (chronicled in the supermarket tabloids) I perceived *The Scream* scratched with fluid, frantic lines, unnerving in their faithfulness to Munch's image, reflecting little shivers of light as I turned the pan and examined it. There are no cosmic accidents in the universe. The pan was a hexagram from the I Ching thrown down. I walked to Ben with it. "Look, it's *The Scream*."

He took a drag off his spliff, reached out for the pan and held it up. "I'll be damned."

"You see it?"

"Duchamp would have lost a screw over this."

"I think it means something."

"Maybe."

"It looks like the apocalypse."

"I can even see Dracula's boat." Ben brought the pan closer to his face, then slowly pulled it back to get another view. He traced the bright silvery waves etched into the pan's surface and then took a draw off his spliff. "Nice piece of work. We'll have to take that with us."

"It might be the spirits. Sending us a message."

We ate breakfast with the sun rising, illuminating the kitchen as we discussed our travel plans and whether the image on the pan was an omen. If we hadn't been followed, then staying for a couple of weeks and taking more time to get our heads on straight and formulate a plan was the preferred solution. If only it weren't for the bills we'd handed over to Mr Connors at the bank. All in all, the pan seemed to herald doom. Was there the possibility of escape, or had fate already tied its noose around our necks? After breakfast, Ben went out to the shed where he'd been working on a disused, unhinged door that had been stacked against the wall outside. He was using oil paints he'd found as well as house paint, turpentine and wood finish, as far as I could tell.

I cleared the breakfast table, fed Hemingway, performed the morning call to the spirits, then wrote for a couple of hours before making a fresh carafe of coffee to take to Ben. On the porch, I saw a vehicle approach and recognized Mr Connors behind the windshield before he got out. Ben went to meet him bare-chested, streaked with aquamarine paint. They conversed; Ben made hand gestures and walked Connors halfway to the front door before turning back for the shed. I held the screened porch door open.

"Hello, Mrs Del Mar. Your husband said he's just got something to finish up and he'll come by. I hope I'm not troubling you."

"No trouble at all, it's wonderful to see you. Come in." I led Mr Connors through the porch where he took a seat, lifted off his hat and sat it on the chair closest to him. I went to the kitchen and came back with a full tray. "I was just on my way to give this carafe to my husband, so I hope you don't mind if I excuse myself for an instant."

"Of course not, Mrs Del Mar." He smiled and took his hat from his knee, then placed it on the chair next to him.

"I'm just going to leave this here." I set a cup down and poured coffee from the carafe for Mr Connors. "Do you take milk, sugar?"

"Thank you, ma'am, just black."

"Please, enjoy the view, and I'll be right back." I walked across the lawn with the tray. Ben was crouched over the door on the ground and had poured turpentine in places over half-dried oil paint, house paint, pieces of broken china, paper collages made from old magazines he'd found, and was directing the streams with a stick through valleys of layered paint and debris. I poured him a cup of coffee.

"I wonder, about Mr Connors being here."

"Yes, I was thinking the same thing. It could be suspicious."

"If it was serious we'd already be surrounded by the Feds."

"Or the mafia."

"I know you know what to do."

"Get as many tells as I can." With that, I went back to Connors on the porch.

"You've got a beautiful animal there," Connors motioned to Hemingway through the screened-in windows, who ran and bounded up and down along the riverbank.

"Yes, he certainly is."

"Well, I just thought I'd come by and see how you folks are getting on. If you needed anything. Enjoying the squirrel hunting?"

"Ben's caught a few. We grilled some the other day. Ate them with beans and fiddleheads. There's a meadow about two miles north of here. I'm sure you know these parts."

"Oh yes. I was born and bred here. I've trekked many a mile through the San Juan foothills."

"Magnificent, these parts."

"I don't want to trouble you two lovebirds –"

"It's no trouble at all. I wasn't doing anything special, as you can see, Ben is off, in the shed. It's nice you came by. Seen any good horror films lately?"

"I don't know, not really. All the new ones are just mostly crap."

"Yeah, I suppose." We sat there, drinking coffee and smoking cigarettes. "You said you grew up in these foothills. Do you know of any old wells not too far from here? Ben and I've been exploring the forest back there. We found a large well. Do you know anything about it?"

"Yeah, I know the place. There are a few of them. Supposedly, they were there even before the Johnsons came. Most likely, the wells were built by some Indian tribe, going way back, maybe for grain. That's the only people who were here, before that." Bud leaned forward a few degrees, locked eyes with me and whispered, "I know this may sound crazy, but I can't help thinking that you're here because you know something, that there's much more to the world than we're led to believe." He made a gesture with his hand and spoke at the normal level. "The evil in the world is more than we can comprehend. It's like a glass shard in my mind, driving me insane. I haven't been able to sleep, well, since about the time you and your husband arrived."

I didn't know what to say. I knew what he was getting at, but it was so abstract I had trouble finding the words. "I know what you're speaking of, yes. And I understand that first there was the *déjà vu*, when you saw us in the bank. Our presence caused some kind of altered mental state in you, psychological or otherwise.

"Then you gave me a clue in your conversation that I was looking for, about Adjani and it was a sign. And now you can't sleep since our arrival. And lastly, I speak of the well. All these instances of synchronicity."

Connors said nothing.

I held his gaze. "I'm looking for my sister, Camille. I heard a sound at the well. It triggered something. A memory of my sister and me coming across a creature like the Mothman. A creature with red hypnotic eyes. Have there been any sightings in these woods?"

"I've heard of it, yes. Our father used to tell us kids about a creature like that. Some people claimed they'd seen it. But not for many, many years. Not since the Sixties. I was a child then. I *do* remember people talking about it." He gave slight nod. "What I know is that people have seen things in the mountains up here. Red, hypnotic lights. If your sister's out there – this thing, you'd never be able to aim and pull the trigger fast enough to hit it. If it even exists."

"I wouldn't want to kill it. I don't know anything about it yet."

"Well, out in the forest, a bear doesn't know much about you does it? Doesn't stop it from killing you. When that thing came around there were some strange happenings going on. It did scare the living daylights out of us, I remember now. Children went missing, three of them. Dogs missing too. Only one adult disappeared, to my knowledge. And you could feel it, there was something, something *not right* and it was all around. Like living in a horror film." He sat back and turned his head toward me. "You know, if you give me something to go on I could try to help you find your sister. I dunno. I grew up with all the boys down at the station here. They do me favours."

"I don't think it's anything they can help me with, Bud, but thanks."

"Don't go out there alone, into the woods at night. If that thing's out there I would think of moving on out of here. Some called that creature a demon from hell."

We both sat there, uneasy. I smoked a cigarette. Mr Connors picked up his hat and rubbed the rim of it with his thumb. "Well, I best be getting on. Leave you two honeymooners to your peace and tranquillity."

"Okay. Well, you're always welcome."

"Thank you for the hospitality."

Connors got up. I followed him to the door and he waved as he walked down the hill to his SUV, then again in Ben's direction before driving off. When I was sure he was gone, I walked down to the shed.

"Baby, could you roll me a spliff?"

"Yeah."

"Well, he wasn't here long."

"I don't think he means us any harm. It seemed more or less like a neighbourly visit. He told me about Mothman sightings here, in the Sixties, and that sound, in the well, it was the same one Camille and I heard, in the Maine woods, when we saw it. I only remembered it just now. The sound brought it back."

"Slow down, baby, *Mothman*?"

"A creature in the woods..." I explained as best I could, about Camille and the messages and how I had been following them as I studied his face, looking for signs.

"Baby, I can tell you that there is no Mothman." He took a drag off his cigarette and stared into nothingness in contemplation. "So, basically he expressed concern for you and warned you about this creature in the woods?"

"He seemed to have come here because he felt compelled to, driven by some inexplicable force."

"So, you mean, he came here for personal reasons and not because he was sent, by say, the bank?"

"Precisely."

"Alright, let's see. We'll need a couple of days to formulate a plan, pack up and head out. We should have enough time to check out that well. I guessed that's where you disappeared to the other night. Please don't do crazy things like that without me ever again."

"I love you."

"Ditto, baby." He sat and drank another cup of coffee. "You look kinda flushed." Ben put his hand to my head. "You're burning up again, Terror. Lay down and I'll bring you some tea. Make you a spliff. You need to rest, baby. You've barely slept since we got here. Go back to the house."

I did as he told me and went to bed. Sheets of static ripped through my head, one after another like ghosts passing through. I stripped the blankets off and got naked.

Perhaps the Mothman "had always been there," like Camille said was the case with the angels. But the angels were madness, a psychotic delusion – that's what they said at the hospital. But we *had* seen the Mothman. Mr Connors knew people who had. Others had seen it too. It was all true. All the signs and symbols, leading me to

Camille. The fever broke in the night. I woke with sweat and salt on my skin and a clear head. I felt wide awake with thoughts gambolling easily and coherently through my head and my vision appeared normal except that Benoît glowed blue under the sheet. My skin was also phosphorescent. Hemingway radiated an eerie canine luminescence. I watched Ben's chest rise and fall with each inhale and exhale of breath.

The radium dial clock read one twenty-three. I opened the window wide enough to slip half out and watched the hot bodies of birds outside make glowing orbs in the canopies while bats blazed with red light, zigzagging against the vault of sky. Every warm-blooded thing around me glowed. I shuddered and remembered a page from my high school diary that went something like:

Take pit-boas and vipers for instance: their vision is more or less like ours, with the added bonus of infrared sensors ten times more sensitive than our most advanced artificial infrared technology. They can switch back and forth from one type of vision to another, or have both views simultaneously. These sensors can even repair themselves. Put me forward for the X-Men experiments.

The ancient Egyptian priests were very careful about what they wrote down. They believed it would come true. Had the words become a spell? What other chains of events had my words set in motion?

It seemed I'd acquired infrared vision, like the pit viper. I was overcome by an incredible thirst and went back inside, drank three glasses of water and afterward examined myself for any other reptilian attributes. Everything appeared normal, except for my glowing skin. I walked into the bedroom where Ben was still sleeping, breathing deeply, his eyes moving in REM sleep, emitting the same glow as before. Hemingway raised his head, half-looked at me, and then set his head back down, his countenance and form changed by the phosphorescence. I got into bed next to Ben, gazing into his face, haloed in a blaze of blue-green radiance. What was happening to me? I decided not to mention this new development to Ben. Things were strange enough already and maybe it would go away, as the electrical charge had. Perhaps when I woke up it would be gone. I fell into a deep sleep.

I woke at the first light of dawn and found that the glow disappeared with the light. I took up a notebook and began to write until Ben awoke, took the pen out of my hand, threw it on the floor and mauled me. He was happy to see I was showing signs of recovery but still wanted me to rest while he saw to my needs and organised our departure.

I couldn't resist going for one of the last swims in the river. I told Ben I would be fine and went with Hemingway, walking to the bank and diving in. Underwater, moving downstream, oscillating patterns of light marked the riverbed corridor and the rocks and reminded me of prehistoric drawings of spirals on the ceiling of the Oracle Chamber in the Hypogeum of Ħal-Saflieni in Malta.

I remembered Camille and me, poring over photographs of the subterranean prehistoric structure carved from solid rock – three levels with more than thirty chambers connected by passages, stairways and halls with trilithons and lintelled doorways. Camille spoke of the astounding acoustic properties of the structure. The bones of seven thousand people were found scattered throughout the Hypogeum, some with elongated skulls, the result of being bound at infancy. Experts believed it to be a necropolis – the first temple of its kind found underground. Camille suspected otherwise, that it was much more than that.

During the excavations, which had begun in 1907 with Sir Temi Zammit, a well-polished, brown clay statue with traces of red ochre in the shape of a bovine woman lying on her side was unearthed. She came to be known as 'The Sleeping Lady of Ħal-Saflieni'. The statue had been found by Zammit in the 'Snake or Votive pit'. To Camille she was undoubtedly a fertility goddess. The figure lay on her side with one hand underneath her cheek, resting on a luxuriant pillow of long flowing hair, gigantic arms pressed against equally ample, exposed breasts. What was a fertility goddess doing in the snake pit of a necropolis? Perhaps the temple was not only for the dead. Perhaps more went on there. Camille believed it was possible the civilization had been as advanced as ours, or even more so, in the sense that they held knowledge of mysteries which would make our hungry, corrupt, corporate world obsolete. It was possible they had developed a technology of the mind, a way of communicating with the forces of nature and walking the righteous path.

Camille had revelled in conjuring up the subterranean scene. She stared at me with her eyes shining. "Imagine the effect of all the people in ceremonial dress, the baritone voices, chanting, with drums and rattles echoing throughout the labyrinth, making the stones vibrate and sing. It would have created a portal into another dimension, another world, a realm of the gods, mustn't it Eugenie?"

Perhaps Malta was the next logical destination. The well may have been a delusion. The Hypogeum seemed the best chance. Breaking and entering the subterranean structure would no doubt prove to be difficult, as it was, and still is, a UNESCO Heritage site. True, I had succeeded at Altamira, but then, the Hypogeum, well, there was only one access point. It was, for all intents and purposes, impenetrable.

Dark clouds began to roll in. I could see neither Hemingway nor Ben. I dove under the water to swim to the bank. All of a sudden there was a great flash – a light so bright I could see nothing else. Then came the boom followed by a shockwave and everything went black.

I found myself floating in the open sea. My body had transmuted into some rarer substance and was as transparent as a heat wave. The sensation was at once terrifying and exhilarating. A four-masted barque with white sails was visible in the distance, heading toward me. As the vessel approached, the air became filled with the sound of drums, chiming and singing and I could see that on the deck were rows of men with the heads of blue jays dressed in turquoise, gold and silver armour, some with staffs and others kneeling, beating on goblet drums. An eagle was tied to the bowsprit. They seemed to be calling for my soul.

I became aware of the presence of creatures moving underneath me in the crepuscular ocean depths, their slippery forms like large komodo dragons with fins, making high-pitched sounds like dolphins or baby crocodiles. These creatures told me they were the true masters of humankind on earth – hence why I could hear them speaking inside of my head. They said they had painstakingly created us and that I had been chosen to receive information the soul usually only acquires after death, if I would just come closer, dive down and follow them... I felt a reptilian appendage with sharp claws around my ankle that jerked my head down below the waterline, pulling me further and further into the fathoms where the exquisite sounds of the blue jay creatures – their voices like singing phosphorescence – could no longer be heard.

The next thing I knew I was floating face-up in a markedly different body of water. It was a river, its surface covered with a thin layer of ash. I breathed in and choked. Above the sky was red and yolky, like a bloodied eye. The reptilians were gone. My sense of a human body had returned to me. I was struck by the realization that I had found myself back in the same river that ran in front of the cabin, only everything had changed. The area had become a wasteland.

A sweet and oily stench – burnt animals and wood – hung heavily in the air. One of my dresses floated by and I swam after it. Clouds of sulphur passed and tumbled downstream above me. I found my spear stuck into the side of the bank and retrieved it. Everything was charred and black for miles. What few trees remained were burnt to cinders, twisted like giant tangles of electrical wire. I climbed up the riverbank and stepped onto dry land. Far off in the distance I made out the tree line encircling the devastated area. After walking maybe five hundred feet I found fragments of what could have been the binoculars, then *The Scream* frying pan. I called to Ben. No response. My blood chilled. No birdcalls, no sign of life. I ran along the river's edge.

Remains of the fireplace came into view. I yelled to Ben and Hemingway until my throat was raw. I followed a trail of utensils. I screamed their names again and again. No answer. I ran further on. An outcropping of boulders appeared with shadows of rabbits in flight burnt onto the surface of the stone. Instinct told me to move out. I had to get downriver, to the tree line. I ran to the riverbank, dove in and stayed underwater for as long as I could, then half swam, half let the current take me, eyeing the stricken land when I came up for breath. Finally, it hit me, the fragrant, forest air. I could breathe deeply again and swam to the riverbank where I pulled myself up and stepped onto dry land, into the warmth and light.

I had the spear. And my white sundress.

I was possessed by a fury and screamed, an animal scream, kneeling on the ground with my head pressed onto the pine needles and dirt, my head on fire, my face wet with tears, punching the earth. Metallic spots boiled in front of my eyes, corroding my vision, burning little bullet holes of blackness through the film strip of my life. I wanted to tear myself apart, immolate myself. The light. It wasn't good. It wasn't a good sign. Ben and Hemingway were gone.

I remember thinking: "Are you watching? You, that created all of this? Are you entertained? Am I doing well? Do you think that I can bear any more?" In this frame of mind, I was very aware that nothing was permanent. Everything was in a state of flux, of vibration, of sound, like the Om, or pure spirit.

How had everything come to this? And then it struck me, the possibility that The Creator was something like Dr Manhattan – the result of some accident, a lone ranger with cosmic powers in a universe, or multiple universes, he struggles to fully comprehend. *Could it be* that the present God or gods are not our actual creators? And are there instead simply beings who usurp the powers of nature to mess with our world on atomic levels, living outside of time, and therefore immortal? Even more disturbing was the distinct possibility that some, or most, of these deities were not acting in our best interests. I was left with a horror that chilled my blood.

I lay on the ground, concentrating on my breathing, and traced a circle in the dirt with a cross in the centre of it. Why had I gone downstream? I should have stayed back there, kept looking. What if by some miracle Ben and Hemingway had survived? I wondered if I should go back. But there was no trace of them, and the rabbits' shadows had been carbonized into the rock, a phenomenon generally made possible by a nuclear explosion. I had survived. Because in atomic blasts, water is your only protection and I had been swimming in it. What would I do without him? I had to follow the signs. Call the spirits. Continue on the path. I had to continue downstream, scour the area, call to him, look for campfires.

I rubbed snot off of my nose with a leaf and sat up. My eyes had swollen. Next to me on the ground lay the spear. I stared up into the trees for a very long time, until angels came pouring out of the canopies, swarming around me, their faces soft with big bleeding-heart eyes. Camille had spoken of angels like these. In fact, there was a time when she had shown them to me. One of them appeared to perform a benediction and kissed me on the forehead. Then they disappeared. Another sign. I could not determine the method in the madness. Each sign led to another without any apparent reason. And yet my life had been heavily influenced by each one. Somehow this trail had brought me to Ben. And now he too was gone. I was in a state of shock.

If the situation and surroundings struck me as being surreal, the cold made itself a palpable presence. I was not dreaming. I had to survive. I had to build a fire and a shelter. I found a pine tree suitable for a lean-to and went about looking for branches to place on top of one another for a wall thick enough to keep the wind out. I collected leaves, bark, pine needles, et cetera, from the forest floor to make a nest inside, then dug a fire pit not far from the entrance. I fashioned a bow from a stick and the hem of my sundress and found a light, dry piece of wood as well as a hard, dense stick for a drill, then a stone with an indent I could use for the socket to make my fire-starting machine. I collected twigs and threw in a bit of my nest for the tinder and found a curved piece of bark for a coal catcher, then went to work building the primitive, yet very effective tool. In no time at all I had a fire going.

From the sky it was nearing six o'clock in the afternoon. I had water, shelter, and fire. Nothing to eat but I wasn't hungry. I had to focus. Surely, if Ben was dead I would be able to feel it. But there was nothing except the constant charge that kept me wide awake, and my alert and racing thoughts, making it difficult to concentrate. I had to meditate, fall into a trance, and invoke the spirits.

My notebooks. They were gone. I would have to rewrite them. But it was all there, in my mind. When I had pen and paper again, I would write it all down.

May 25th, Sunshine Pass environs, Colorado

The icy blackness of space ... stars glittering diamond hard, twinkling at me ... codes ... light years ringing in my ears ... look at this tangle of thorns ...

Frost was on the ground. I circled the fire, watching it, waiting for the sun to rise. The stars were possessed of a brightness that was almost painful, boring into my head. I couldn't sleep. Dream yoga would have been an appropriate action to take but was far beyond my reach. I moved around the fire.

Who knew what was out there? What experiment had gone awry? I could be dealing with anything. The flash of light. Everything ended with the flash of light. Perhaps I too was dead, or Ben was out there, deposited with Hemingway further on in the forest, in which case, I should be trying to focus on remote viewing. The Mothman could be out there too, somewhere. I hadn't heard him and I hadn't seen any signs from Camille. Pink light shone through the cloud cover and illuminated the forest. I felt encased in a globe. Snow began to fall. Mist rose from the forest floor. I lay beside the fire, closed my eyes and repeated what I remembered from the Nine Purifications breathing practices. Every now and then I attempted to initiate the remote viewing process with no success. I couldn't get my mind clear or calm enough.

Eventually I stood up, blood rushing to my head so that I sat back down and waited for the malaise to pass. When it had gone, I took the spear, rose to my feet and made my way to the riverbank. From a rise in the terrain, I stopped and watched the light hit the surrounding peaks and splintered crests of the giant San Juan Mountains. The greatest peak held a crimson hue for what seemed like an hour at least. I imagined its crags, caverns and abysses, its very form, influencing the weather, chaining the strong winds and then letting them loose in its fury with the forked lightning playing round its head like a celestial crown. I then continued on my way, picking some small, dark red berries and wondering if they were poisonous.

The fish were abundant. I wasn't hungry but felt compelled to catch one of them and make myself eat. I caught three with little effort, brained them each on a rock and carried them up the hill to the lean-to and the fire. Then I saw him. The Mothman – hovering above the ground with the last light of the sun illuminating his great, moth-like wings, gaudily spotted with gold, gathering snow. In the daylight his eyes barely glowed, but I felt the force of their hypnotic powers firmly on my forehead, pulling me in, distorting my thoughts. I couldn't move. It was impossible to tell how much time had passed before I felt like I had 'come to' and looked into the face of this creature, furry like a gigantic Emperor Gum Moth. I don't know why but I held the fish out. A great tongue (like a long, thin leech) shot out and wrapped around my hand, taking the fish with it on its whip-like retreat. I watched him swallow.

"Do you know Camille? A girl who looks like me?" I took another fish by the tail and threw it to him. The creature's tongue whipped out again and caught the glistening, slippery body in mid-air. "Please, take me to her." I held up the last fish and felt the rough edge of his tongue, like a cat's, as he took it. The creature then rose up perhaps twelve feet into the air, creating an influx of wind so powerful I found myself hovering above the ground. We went off like a shot, darting between the wide girths of the ponderosas, over meadows, through groves of birch, along the riverbank, through tunnels of willows. When we came to an area populated with aspen we slowed and stopped at a well, much like the one I had seen before, with Benoît and Hemingway that day in the forest. It was full with clear, ruby-red water. Steam rose from it. The Mothman left me at the edge and disappeared into the wilderness.

I took as much air into my lungs as I could, stepped up onto the stone ledge and dove in. The water was warm and the thermal viper vision made everything appear lit up like in a darkroom. Ten-foot-long koi glided past, spotted with black marks. I swam until my breath told me I would have to turn around and at the last moment came to a hole in the ceiling, like an ice fishing hole. I grabbed the edges and pulled myself through it, gasping.

Human bones were laid out haphazardly on the ground. The entire room had been carved out of limestone and was lit by a fireplace at the far end. I went to it, laid my spear against the wall, squeezed my dress out and hung it from the spear to dry. Three trilithon doorways, tilted slightly in opposing directions, led to other chambers lit by fire. Above was a balustrade, suggesting another level. Had I found myself at the Hypogeum of Hal-Saflieni? Or a structure very much like it? All around were bones scattered on the dirt floor and little niches in the walls with primitive oil lamps in them. I went through the central doorway, walked down a passage and came to the next chamber with the same curved walls and corbelled limestone ceilings from which hung garlands of skulls and bones that gathered in the centre and fell into an intricate chandelier where candles burned on pelvises turned upward like lotus flowers that held human skulls.

Asleep in layers of white pelts atop a slab of limestone in the centre of the room was Camille. Roses, clumps of violets and forget-me-nots lay on the floor and all around her on the altar. A chain of daisies crowned her head. I watched her, breathing deeply, and stroked her hair. Tears rolled down my face. She was flesh. I kissed her pale cheek and whispered her name. Camille's eyes opened. She looked at me, drowsily.

"Camille, I've been looking for you."

"Eugenie?" Her eyes brightened, she sat up, legs folded underneath her. "I hoped you would find the way here. I've missed you terribly, Eugenie. You're naked. Take my cloak." She slipped the garment from her shoulders and handed it to me. I wrapped myself in the soft fur and got up onto the limestone beside her. We held one another and convulsed into tears. "How did we get separated?"

"It was just after we doused Dr V's clothes in mother's perfume and he was attacked by the killer bees. I thought he was dead, but in fact, he is still alive."

"I thought as much."

"So, when shall we go? Do you know how to get out of here?"

"Eugenie, we can't stay here, together. In fact, you're in danger of becoming trapped if you stay too long. What I have to tell you is this –"

"What do you mean?"

"It's very complicated. I called you here because there's something you have to see."

"Will we never be together, ever again?"

"We *will* meet again. What you must do now is pass through that archway, into the next chamber you see. There you will wait until a creature or a man appears. This is the Oracle. You will be given a gift. It is a gateway, like I had always imagined, only far beyond my wildest dreams."

"Are you a prisoner here?"

"I was taken unawares by the Lord of the Underworld. He fell in love with me and made me his bride. So I now dwell here, and in many other places underground, wherever he wishes me."

"This can't be true."

"It is."

"What can I do? Could the Oracle help us?"

"Anything is possible but it is doubtful. I'm under the Lord of the Underworld's spell. He has made the rules in my case. The Oracle doesn't often meddle in his affairs, it's too dangerous."

"So, is there nothing I can do?"

"Sister, I do not dare tell you what act would lift this curse."

"Tell me."

"I cannot."

"You must tell me, Camille. What is this terrible thing that must be done?"

"My Lord, the one who possesses me, has cast a spell that I shall not be free until the day you kill me like a sacrifice, cut my throat, then eat a piece of my flesh. This act would free me, if his words are to be trusted, for he does not always tell the truth and he does not always lie. He likes to play with fire.

"I have no bearings on where I am. I am not even sure whether this figure before you is 'me' or a hologram I can somehow 'experience' and my true self is somewhere else entirely."

"Camille, this is madness." I touched her soft cheek.

"You'll see. It's not." She reached underneath a clump of roses and pulled out a knife – "Remember it's a dream, just a dream" – then handed the blade to me, her eyes brave and bright. "I've taken a good dose of the poppies. I won't feel a thing. Take this and do it. You must."

I saw there was no other way and took the knife from her hand. Camille turned her pale, slender neck to me. I slit her throat. Blood from the jugular sprayed out, all over me, all over everything as I held her limp body and laid it down on the altar, blood coursing out with the last beats of her heart. I cut a piece of flesh from her side and ate it.

Then, there was nothing. Camille was gone and I felt nothing at all, except a menacing numbness. I went through the doorway she had indicated, the way to the Oracle. In this chamber, the ceilings were corbelled into a conic shape like a beehive or a bell. The place was empty. I sat and waited. I felt sick. I kept telling myself it was all a dream. I was in a dream and would wake up at any moment.

The Mothman, or a creature of the same species, came through the doorway, hovering about two feet off the ground, humming in a deep baritone that sounded like chanting. The walls began to reverberate, so much so that I could feel it in my bones. The room and all that it contained smeared into a hot blur. Everything went up in flames. My body was torn to pieces, my teeth and bones broken to fragments. A clarity and euphoria swooped down and carried me up, sailing through the cosmos in what seemed to be an angelic form. Voices spoke to me. Voices like rivers and the hissing sound of the wind through canopies of leaves.

Then I awoke.

Everything was bright – Benoît's face came out of the light. The sun stung my eyes. "Baby doll, I knew you'd pull through." He kissed me on the lips.

"I had a dream –"

"Terror, you've been out for forty-eight hours. I had Travis call a doctor. He said to just let you rest. You have a concussion. You hit your head on a rock."

"It was like a real-life place. I thought I'd lost you."

"I'm not going anywhere without you, baby. You should know that by now."

May 27th–30th, Sunshine Pass environs, Colorado

The following days were dominated by the sweetness of spring. Much time had passed since we arrived in town and carelessly deposited five hundred dollars of our casino winnings in the General Bank in exchange for a gun and chequebook and yet nothing had happened – no FBI agents or Mafiosi had encircled the cabin and moved in. We reckoned there was a good chance we were safe. Perhaps we had succeeded in hiding ourselves. I had carved a Norse symbol, Hulinhjálmur, for concealment and invisibility on sticks and pushed them into the ground around the outside of the house to the north, south, east, and west appealing to the deities to protect us. Perhaps they were working.

When we further assessed the situation, there was no real way of knowing if we had used marked bills from the last casino where we held the two men at gunpoint, or whether the money had been from a previous one where no crime had been committed. The law of averages pointed to the money we used being clean. We wondered whether it was safer to stay in one place, or find another hideout somewhere in another state. The finding of the frying pan with the depiction of *The Scream* entered the conversation. I cautioned it might be a portent. Benoît said he wasn't finished with America yet.

After the accident it felt as though another obscuring layer had been corroded. Things were beginning to become clearer. I'd found Camille, as I suspected, in another realm. She was being held prisoner by one of the supernatural beings there – the Lord of the Underworld, no less. In our childhood and adolescence we had performed ceremonies and vowed to sacrifice ourselves to these unearthly beings in exchange for the death of Dr V, but he was still alive, and Camille had been made a prisoner. Clearly we had failed in our mission. We were out of our depth.

But what other path could we have taken? The occasions the two of us had surpassed what is normally thought humanly possible – precognition, mind reading, becoming invisible, calling hailstorms, et cetera – were shining portents that led us on. In the end we hadn't managed to maintain any real control over any of these powers and the proof was that we had not eradicated Dr V. The encounter with Camille had been all too real – I shuddered to think of it. I had to assume she was free now and when she could, she would contact me.

I knew full well what we had embarked upon so long ago was treacherous. Camille warned me at every turn of the danger and told stories of other seekers who had fallen to fates worse than death. But if we were going down, it would be fighting. Success equalled the end of Dr V and one less evil in the world. It also contained the possibility of gaining more knowledge than an ordinary life could offer.

At the core, our incurably curious natures were difficult to contain – inquiring minds want to know. We were intent on living to the fullest capacity. Within the dangers hid the thrill and the possibility of a greater enlightenment. I couldn't stop now, especially since it might be the only means of finding Camille.

Nearly every night before bed, Camille read to me through the ventilation shaft that connected our rooms. William S. Burroughs was one with *The Place of Dead Roads* being the most memorable. The novel chronicled the life of a homosexual gunfighter in the Wild West, beginning with his death and making use of Burroughs' extensive knowledge of weaponry and the occult. He had us rolling on the floor in fits of laughter. Then there was Henry James's *Turn of the Screw*, Nabokov's *Ada or Ardor*, Homer's *Odyssey*, the list goes on. Jack Kerouac's *On the Road* was yet another. There is one line I will never forget: "... the only people for me are the mad ones, the ones who are mad to live, mad to talk, mad to be saved, desirous of everything at the same time, the ones who never yawn or say a commonplace thing, but burn, burn, burn like fabulous yellow roman candles exploding like spiders across the stars." I could hear in Camille's voice how her eyes shone as she intoned life into the words, inhabiting the characters and the wild abandon of Kerouac's prose as all moved toward the kind of sacred symmetry one finds in a great jazz improvisation. Camille had captured all of this. I had never known anyone who burned as brightly as Camille. Once, in one of her trances, she had said that all was a manoeuvre of shadow and light, that you had to dodge and you had to burn until you held the vision, as Ansel Adams had done with his photographs. There was no time to waste; we were in the pursuit of masterpieces.

Benoît and I smoked more marijuana than I'd ever smoked in my life. We tried making hash but found it was too time consuming and much of the pitch stuck to our fingers, which in the end was annoying.

There was an incredible amount of sex. By the end Benoît looked like he'd been punched in the face. He spent lot of time resting, which left me to practise gymnastics, swim in the river, draw, collect feathers and rocks in the forest to make offerings, shadow box, climb trees, practise with my pendulum (it responded to the rate of dead animals at twenty inches, at ten was light, fire, sun, red, east, graphite and truth), et cetera, et cetera. I felt little need for sleep and did a lot of writing. It was as though I had tapped into an enormous energy source. I called the spirits each dawn. The visions of phosphorescence or the infrared vision came and went. Sometimes I was able to change between the two types of vision.

The fact that we couldn't stay there forever pressed on us with each passing day. There were long discussions about Hemingway's welfare. It seemed selfish to take him out of the country. Ben had brought his dog Gisele on the road with him until she was stolen, but it wasn't a life for Hemingway. He needed security and something stable. If we went to Canada we could take him there. Mexico and South America would be too hot unless we went up into the mountains. We didn't want to put him through a cross-continental airplane trip and uncertainty afterward. With heavy hearts we knew Hemingway had to stay. We would have to ask Travis. He seemed to have taken a shine to the dog. We were almost certain he would be happy to have him. The next time we saw him he would have to ask him.

I told Ben about the money in Maine, hidden within my mother's childhood home, last I heard occupied by Dr V. We could infiltrate, get the cash, then come back for Hemingway and disappear into the woods like Travis suggested. We could still go to raves. He had his records, he could DJ and we could make a studio here. Maybe we could go to New Mexico.

"Sure, baby. We could do it."

I did not know what to say. I questioned whether I had actually proposed the plan to Ben out loud. But I had, and he'd accepted. I knew that a long road lay ahead, and saw in his eyes that he knew too. "Come here, *mon cœur.*" He took me by the hand and pulled me to him, taking my face in his hands. "It's my duty to eradicate this demon from the face of the earth. It was part of my plan all along. You know I couldn't leave this country without annihilating him."

"No, I didn't know you felt that way."

"If you say there's money there on top of it all, well, that's the cherry on the cake."

"I love you."

"Ditto."

It was settled. We would stay until we had a plan to rob Vargas. Then we would either return to these mountains or leave the country.

May 31ˢᵗ–June 3ʳᵈ, Sunshine Pass environs, Colorado

Ben painted outside in the natural light while I wrote on the porch and reread passages from a book I'd found at a Parisian bookshop before we left for Las Vegas entitled *The Cosmic Serpent: DNA and the Origins of Knowledge*, by a social anthropologist called Jeremy Narby. The snake on the cover had drawn me in. Since the viper bite the notion DNA was in fact, among other things, a radio tower emitting signals, haunted me. Camille believed that DNA in no matter what form – be it a butterfly, a dog, a human, a tree, a virus – communicated across all categories of living organisms. In this way, a human could theoretically share knowledge with an owl, a tree, a fish, et cetera. Narby's work added credence to Camille's hypothesis, presenting evidence that in specific mental states a person can communicate with other forms of life via DNA.

Narby carried out his research in the Peruvian Amazon where he was initiated into the realm of the *ayahuasqueros*, healers, or medicine men among other names. Through the ingestion of the psychotropic brew *ayahuasca* and speaking to these men of knowledge, he collected information and consulted with a biochemist to reach his theory that, in short, DNA communicates through biophotons. This was how the medicine men through the ages had gained their knowledge, through the exchange of particles of light.

I remembered Camille telling me that in 1880 Alexander Graham Bell and Charles Sumner Tainter invented the Photophone, a device to transmit voice signals over an optical beam. NASA had used fibre optics in the television cameras they sent to the moon. Here again, information travelled through photons, through light beams. Why wouldn't they also travel through biophotons?

The medicine men Jeremy Narby spent time researching in the Peruvian jungle knew countless combinations of plants. Out of the 250,000 or more varieties, they knew which combinations cured countless numbers of remedies. Over ninety percent of Western pharmaceuticals are based on chemical combinations found in the plant combinations the indigenous Amazonian people had been using for millennia. (Narby was a witness to this medicine. He had a chronic back problem at the time, took one of the medicine man's remedies and over seven years later had not had another recurrence of the problem.)

Part of Narby's mission was to gather evidence that the native people of the area used all that was left of the jungle that surrounded them (what the lumber companies had not yet cut down) for their survival and the survival of their culture so that the people and the land could be protected by law. Reading the book also made me think that I was leading a selfish life. I should be dedicating myself to a noble cause. But first I had to find Camille. Then we could make plans.

Ben read *The Mysteries of Udolpho* to me in bed, brought me tea and spliffs and we would inevitably make love all afternoon. Many times it occurred to me that I had died. But then something would click and I would know I was alive, and that Dr V was as well and that Ben and I had made a pact to go after him. Icicles sounded like the best bet. People were killed by icicles all of the time in Maine. If the armed guards with their semi-automatics and rifles hadn't been let go things were going to be more difficult. There wasn't anyone I could telephone to provide me with this information without arousing suspicion, and taking an incalculable risk. Remote viewing seemed the safest possibility to retrieve the kind of information I sought. I spent hours each day in practice until I was able to focus on my target – the great house in the Maine woods, what I believed to be Dr V's current lair. To begin the exercise, I lay down on the bed with eyes closed and performed breathing exercises in an effort to calm the blizzard of electrical stimulation, so that the brain can reach the quiescent state of theta where remote viewing is possible.

The next step was to pick up the signal line, or transmission of energy, emanating from the target, in this case, the estate in Maine. After two days of these mental exercises and meditation I managed to reach the grounds surrounding the great edifice with the scents and sounds of the wood winding me round with their familiar, intoxicating presence. When I got to the guards' huts, the mark of Dr V's perfection was present in the way everything had been arranged. The rooms appeared abandoned. I had achieved the first signal line. My next move was to the main house, where I believed the Doctor was lurking.

In the remote viewing process, whatever occurs during the time you're under is sent to the subconscious in code, so that the information, or recall, cannot be accessed easily while in the state of 'everyday reality'. Fragments of what happened there resurface, often prompted by certain sounds or acts. Having a pencil and a piece of paper handy is often the best means to get information quickly. When I emerged from the remote viewing session I saw that I had drawn symbols on the piece of paper in front of me which indicated the guards were no longer at the scene. My previous training in captivity must have allowed me to perform such a feat. It took practice to be able to write or draw in that state, and it would seem that it was like riding a bike. I'd retrieved the first piece of information I had gone in for. Benoît was not entirely convinced until I told him about remote viewing's success in the United States military. That won him over.

How much longer to remain at the cabin? This question kept coming back through days that seemed incredibly drawn out yet, ultimately, too short. I tended to think we should leave sooner; Benoît, later. He wanted to remain longer to have ample time to consult Travis, who at the very least seemed to know the lay and laws of the land, which was more than we knew. I began to have the feeling we would end our days in these foothills, which is perhaps the best way to live, like it might be your last.

December 24th, Passamaquoddy Bay Region, Maine

Maynard put the notebook down. He decided he would go to the Vargas estate to see what, exactly, was going on. Nothing had been reported on the CB radio.

The notebooks were very peculiar, to say the least. They made him feel strange and brought the taste of metal to his mouth. Maynard noticed his heart beating faster. The storm was only going to get worse. He began to make mental notes of what he would need.

Could the notebooks have been written by Eugenie Lund, the missing heiress? Did she have a sister? Maynard struggled to remember any information on the case, anything he'd read in newspapers or heard on the radio. Nothing came to him, just a feeling that somehow, he was connected. He picked up the shotgun and also took a Beretta. Brigitte was at the door before he had his coat on. The flakes had grown into large clusters but it was still very bright out. Through the snow-laden trees, it appeared as though three suns burned in the haze with orbs around them. A sundog. Maynard recalled hearing that the Indians regarded them as a good omen.

The beauty of the forest, covered in snow, was not lost on Maynard. He loved these parts and the deep woods surrounding the cabin. There were roughly a thousand acres between his and the Vargas property. He would walk down the path to where his truck was parked then swing it round along the public road off which was the unassuming entrance onto the long, winding drive that ran to Vargas's gates. The only other way was through the forest, which would require snowshoes and take a hell of a lot longer. Both ways were dangerous, with one being much faster. Brigitte bounded ahead and disappeared, eventually circling around to find her master again. All sounds were deadened in the snow, like in a tunnel made of earth, or a tomb. It was comforting, peaceful somehow. The truck stood covered with at least three inches of the stuff. He had installed chains on the front tyres the day before in anticipation of the storm and had also put the plough on. Maynard pushed snow off the front and back windshields with his arm, then turned the engine on, got an ice scraper and finished the job. Brigitte took a running leap into the cab once it had heated up.

After empty stretches of road with thick forest on either side, everything was covered in white, with the visibility greatly diminished. Maynard turned off onto the long dirt drive that led to the Vargas estate. He followed it through the wood until he met with a wrought iron gate, ten feet tall, and got out of his truck to push on it. The gate opened. He got back into the truck and continued down the drive with Brigitte looking thoughtfully out the side window until pieces of the great house appeared through the trees.

The drive curved and descended behind the edifice where there was a garage and a white Mitsubishi Montero sat backed up against a snow bank. Maynard parked, took the shotgun and got out of the car, holding the door so that Brigitte could jump down into the snow. He scanned the area. Further down the hill, through the trees, he could make out a white clapboard cottage.

A small staircase from the drive led to a granite terrace, which led to another staircase and a back door. Maynard climbed the steps, got to the top and turned the knob. It opened. He and Brigitte stepped inside and found themselves in a kitchen half the size of a ballroom with a black and white marble checkerboard floor. Gothic windows cast faint silos of light on the tiles with the shadows of the pines moving back and forth in the wind like pendulums. Maynard locked the door and stood as quietly as he could with Brigitte beside him, both of them listening for any movement. The place reeked of old money.

Brigitte put her nose to the floor and led him through a swinging door that opened to a dining room with red wallpaper and a crystal chandelier hanging above a heavy, dark wood table. Palms erupted out of large Chinese vases at all corners of the room. Broken pieces of a tea set lay on the floor. They went through the door at the other side and were met with a smoking room where framed and mounted rocks with prehistoric figures and paintings of monsters hung on the walls. The next door opened onto a hallway, which led to a marble entrance hall with a red oriental carpet running up the grand staircase. Two stuffed bears stood on the landing with crystal lamps shining from their open jaws.

They crossed the entrance hall. Brigitte turned right down another corridor and stopped in front of a closet. Inside were mostly coats. A thin ray of light came from the back where, instead of a wall, there was a door ajar. Stone steps led underground. Maynard noticed drops of blood. The place looked like a bunker. He told Brigitte to sit and wait outside in the hall and then descended.

There, in the hallway, was the girl. It was her, Eugenie. Beside her was the dog that looked like a wolf described in the notebooks.

"It's you."

"I don't know who you think I am, Eugenie, it is Eugenie, isn't it?"

"Yes."

"Eugenie Lund?"

"Yes."

"I came to help you."

"I knew you would come." Her eyes shone.

"Do you need help?"

She nodded. "Yes, I suppose."

"It's the Doctor, isn't it?"

"We stabbed him with icicles but it barely made a difference. He's like Rasputin. We've had to resort to other ways of killing him." She turned her head and motioned with her hand. "He's down there, tied up, with my husband watching over him."

"Look, I'll just run it by you straight. I don't want any blood on your hands, Eugenie. It isn't necessary. Mine are *bloody enough. Your husband is no doubt capable of taking care of it on his own but I have,"* he paused, *"experience."*

"I don't think he would let you do it. You've come too late. It's a vendetta for him now." The girl was certainly beautiful, even then, in those moments of horror. Her lips were red as blood, her hair dark, like ink, her skin pale, luminescent. The whole situation seemed nearly impossible. She tilted her head upward to see his face better. *"I know what you've come to do, and I do appreciate it."*

Maynard thought she looked like a child, a waif, no older than sixteen, with a face like a cherub. He didn't know whether she made him feel sad or inspired something in him. It was probably both. One thing was certain, she needed help. She needed to get back to her father. Back to her family. He was going to do everything within his power to make that happen.

A door opened on the corridor and a man stepped out, Eugenie's husband. *"Ce qui se passe ici?"*

"It's okay, mon amour. We can trust him. I know him from when I was a little girl. He's come to take care of it. It's what he's here to do."

"Take care of what?"

"He knows, he knows everything. He's the man in the woods from the visions I told you about, with Camille."

Maynard didn't wait for introductions. He passed Eugenie and stood in front of her husband. *"Let me have a crack at him."*

The Frenchman looked Maynard in the eye, then at his wife, and back again at Maynard. *"Okay but don't kill him."* The husband opened the door and Maynard stepped in, closing the door behind him. Vargas was unconscious, bleeding from his side and chest, slumped over, tied to a wooden chair. A circle of blood had been drawn around him as well as symbols Maynard didn't recognise.

It was one hell of a day. He struggled to remember how it had come to this. The blood on the snow, the strange notebooks. The girl. Her husband. Maynard now had confirmation; she was the missing heiress. He advanced toward Vargas. The Doctor's skin was sallow, his eyes seemingly bruised shut. Upon Maynard's approach the eyelids flickered. He leaned in slowly and saw that Vargas could perceive him – there was still intelligence lurking. "I see you've come," the Doctor spoke as though he were a ventriloquist, barely moving his lips.

"I don't know what you're talking about, old man."

"I have money. Let me go and you will be rewarded."

"If I don't kill you, they will."

"I just want to be let go. That's all I'm asking. I just want another chance." The Doctor sat motionless.

"You won't survive them. I'm just here to save the girl the trouble. She's already been through enough."

"If you take the vial, sewn in the trouser cuff, and make me drink it, you will see."

"What have you done with the sister, Camille?"

"She doesn't have one. She's a schizophrenic. Camille is imaginary."

"I see."

"So you see that she is mentally unstable and needs help. I can help her. I'm a doctor, a psychiatrist, as you may know."

"You know, I don't think I'm going to be getting any useful information out of you. Now, I'm going to give you several options to meet your death and you choose which one you prefer. Number one, knife to the throat, two, Beretta, or three, hanging. I saw some rope over there in the corner. You're lucky. If you had met me in my twenties your guts would be like a firehose in my hands by now while we were having a different kind of conversation. And here, I'm giving you a choice."

"You drive a hard bargain."

"Or I could throw kerosene all over you and light a match on my way out."

"Yes. Purified by fire."

Maynard set the shotgun against a display case, took a knife from his belt and slit Vargas's throat. The Doctor made an unearthly sound, gurgling in his blood – "Tell her" – and slumped over, inanimate. It was then Maynard realised that from the moment he'd entered the room he'd had the sensation of hands around his throat, of being slowly strangled, until he slit the Doctor's offending throat with the knife. Immediately after, he could breathe freely and easily again. Blood spatter covered his face and was all over the floor, extending beyond the circle of blood that had been drawn by Eugenie and her husband.

In times like these, it was best not to try to make too much sense of it all. The present called for the tactics of survival. He turned to collect his shotgun, then walked out of the room and climbed the stairs to find Brigitte waiting for him opposite the closet door. They found Eugenie, her husband and their dog in the entrance hall. "It's done. Now we all have to find gasoline, anything flammable. It's got to go up in flames."

Eugenie sat on the staircase and looked down upon Maynard between the balusters. "Yes, I know where we can find something like that, but did you say he was dead?"

"Yes."

"You son of a bitch." The Frenchman had the shine of savagery in his eyes and made his way across the hall toward Maynard. Brigitte crouched, hairs on her back raised, teeth gnashing in front of the advancing threat to her master, while the girl descended the staircase at an even pace and stopped well above the standoff. The wolfish one had immediately moved into position in front of Brigitte, both animals growling and gnashing teeth, snapping at each other's muzzle, engaged in a vicious, electric, terrifying show of menace that quickly turned into a full attack despite efforts to call them off. There was blood but soon the dogs were pulled apart and taken to separate spots on either side of the stairwell where their panting, saliva-wet, bloodied bodies were gone over for injuries. Both parties discovered they could hear one another if they spoke just slightly louder than usual.

"Mine's fine, just a few places where the skin broke. How's yours?" The Frenchman called to Maynard.

"No harm done. So what do we do now?" Maynard held Brigitte by the collar while she lay next to him, still panting with her head on his lap.

"He was going to tell us where he had stashed a lot of cash in a safe and the combination. That's why I specifically told you not to kill him. So please, say it isn't so, you're making a very bad joke."

"I'm pretty sure he's dead. But go see for yourself. I've got a hold of my dog. Go and see."

"All right then." The Frenchman kissed his wife, told his dog to stay and walked across the hall, passing Maynard and his dog on his way to the basement to discover the truth of the matter at hand. He made his way down the steps and into the corridor and at that moment everything felt surreal. Getting a code to a safe seemed irrelevant. Benoît turned in through the open doorway and stood in the brightly lit room before the slumped figure with blood sprayed across its face, soaked from the neck down. The Doctor was dead.

In all fairness, they'd done a good job. They'd accomplished what they'd set out to. There was nothing more but to loot the house and make a clean getaway. No time to cry over spilt milk. He came up the steps into the hall and went directly to speak to Maynard, to make peace. If peace couldn't be achieved, the whole operation would easily fuck up. They were already pressed for time, and in fact were even in the danger zone with the blizzard that had begun outside. There wasn't any room for conflict in the equation for a safe getaway. Ben left the dead man and mounted the stairs, then walked down the corridor toward Maynard.

Maynard was the first to speak. "I didn't come to stop you. I came to help. I apologise for killing him. I should have listened to you. Something came over me."

"Apology accepted. The main thing is, he's dead." The Frenchman paused and looked into Maynard's eyes, unflinching. "There's more money in here, besides the safe, there's maybe a few hundred grand hidden under the floorboards. Help us find it and we'll split it three ways."

"You do know she's an heiress, a missing heiress, from a prominent American family. Her father's been searching for her for years. He offered a reward of two million dollars a while back for any information leading to her safe return."

The Frenchman maintained his composure. "What do you mean to do? Turn her over to her father? I'm her husband. I'm taking care of her now. She and I, and now you, are going to find the piles of cash, burn the place down and scatter with the wind."

"It's not why I came. It was for other reasons. Maybe I shouldn't have. It looks like all I've done is complicate matters. I apologise. I'll help you find the cash. I didn't mean to rock the boat. I don't want a cut of anything."

"I don't think you came here for the wrong reasons. I'm pretty good at reading a man."

"Like I said, I'm here to help."

"Okay, then we reintroduce the dogs." The Frenchman called to his wife, "Genie, baby, I'm coming with the man and his dog. Bring Hemingway out into the main hall. We've going to make friends."

"Alright, I'm heading down the corridor with Hemingway."

Shortly after the girl's reply the four met at the centre of the entrance hall with roughly five feet between them. Maynard had used his belt to make a short lead for Brigitte and Hemingway was on a rope tied to his collar. Both parties met in the middle with the dogs under control so that they could gaze at and eventually approach one another with coaxing from their masters until they accepted each other and were let off the leash to go about their own business. There wasn't any playful interaction between them; it was more of a mutual respect from there on.

The three went to work, the men with nail pullers and pry bars while Eugenie walked from room to room tapping on the floorboards, humming in a way Maynard had never heard before, struggling even to put a name to the sound she produced. In just shy of twenty minutes she had found nearly three hundred grand this way. Safes in hidden cupboards and secret rooms were discovered but the codes and the safes themselves were too difficult to break.

Maynard took it into full consideration that he had embarked on a doomed enterprise, one that would cause him to look back and curse himself. He had murdered a man and was now aiding and abetting two people carrying out a B&E. Then he would commit arson. It wasn't the first time he'd done something well above and beyond the law. The law stopped making sense to him a long time ago. However, matters were further complicated by the fact that one of the parties involved was a famous missing person, something he did not want to even brush shoulders with, much less attach himself to. If she were ever found and placed him in the spotlight it would all be over. His life depended on living under the radar, untraceable, like a shadow. To be connected to a case like this, something that could easily turn into a cause célèbre, was the last thing Maynard wanted on God's green earth. He would help them on their way and disappear.

In under an hour they had finished taking all they wanted from the house, poured gasoline over everything and lit matches. Maynard waited for the couple in his truck with the engine on and could smell the burning of wood and petrol. Flames appeared out of several windows. The couple emerged and the girl waved as she walked past on her way to their vehicle, while the Frenchman went to Maynard's truck where they spoke through the rolled-down window. "This is for you to keep quiet. You'll not speak of me; I'll not speak of you." He handed Maynard a stack of bills.

"That suits me fine. We never met."

The two parties parted ways, leaving the burning house behind, each taking a different direction after they came to the main road. The snowfall had increased. Anyone without chains on their tyres wasn't going very far. He thought he should have insisted they return with him to the cabin and wait the storm out. But that would entail more risk. He'd meddled enough. Best to make a quick exit. He did not want to make the mistake of becoming further involved. He told himself it was a dream, that it had never happened. The snow and the fire would hopefully take care of the evidence. He would keep his ears on the police radio. His alibi was reasonable and he would, first thing when he got back, hide the backpack somewhere it could not be found. He had forgotten to tell Eugenie he had her backpack with the notebooks, and the stack of bills, that it was all in his possession, in his truck. How had he not given it to her? Had the encounter rattled him that much?

Maynard turned the vehicle around and headed in the direction the couple had taken. He reasoned they hadn't gotten far, but they were nowhere to be seen. Beyond the windshield was the road in the headlights and the mesmerizing white specks falling and dancing on the blackness of the night. He drove like this for fifteen minutes, then turned around and headed back to the cabin, calculating when his turn off would be. The visibility became nil; there was no way he'd see his exit without being precise. Then the deer hit – a buck through the glass, its antler piercing Maynard's chest, deep into the heart. The vehicle flipped over. All three died in the wreckage, in the falling snow.

New Clue to Missing Heiress Found in a Dead Maine Man's Car Wreck
BY DIEGO KERKHOF August 6, 19-

A man who has been identified as Maynard Grady was found dead off a major route due to a motor accident with a deer in which he was fatally stabbed by an antler. In his possession at the time of death were notebooks which handwriting analysts have determined belong to the missing heiress Eugenie Lund. Her father, Erik Lund, head of his late father's publishing empire and Arctic explorer, has renewed his search for his missing daughter and announced that the $2m reward for information leading to her safe return is still being offered.

Sightings of Eugenie Lund have been reported from nearly every state across the country. Leads are being followed but progress is slow due to the sheer number of people calling tip hotlines in a frenzy that is acting to further obscure her whereabouts. Many believe she has left the country.

The notebooks found in the mangled car belonging to Maynard Grady contain a memoir detailing her wedding and honeymoon with a Frenchman, beginning in Las Vegas and ending in Colorado. How much of the tale is true is yet to be substantiated.

The link between Eugenie Lund and Maynard Grady remains a mystery. Investigators are trying to determine whether Grady was involved in a case of murder and arson which occurred several hours before his death near to where his body was found. The identity of the murder victim has yet to be released. And so, the hunt for the missing heiress continues.

Come home, Eugenie, your father misses you.

Acknowledgements

Many factors were at play in the creation of this novel. There's a famous story about Pablo Picasso and a napkin on which he'd made a drawing in thirty seconds and then told the man who had wanted to buy it that it cost a million dollars. The man thought it ludicrous to pay so much for something that had taken so little time. Picasso replied that it had taken all his years of work to be able to create the drawing. And that is how it is with this novel, and most likely all novels. It would take at least another novel to acknowledge all of the forces that acted to create it.

Dodge and Burn began as a short story I left unfinished and put away when I became heavily involved in writing a road trip novel for my degree final project at Kingston University, London. The short story was a recollection of a short story I had written when I was seventeen – an attempt at magical realism with a maleficent Dr. Vargas, an attack of killer bees, and a heroine who may or may not have succumbed to insanity. Time was running out for a module in experimental fiction I had neglected, so I had no choice but to expand and modify the short story to fit the expected assignment. It turned out to be the best piece I'd ever written. The story and characters haunted me enough to make me dig in and turn it into a novel.

There are many people who've helped me along the way, many kind souls I'd like to thank whose names I've forgotten, strangers who picked me up hitch-hiking and took me in and put up with me, cured me of pneumonia, from poisoning by contaminated water, and monoxide poisoning on the way to a festival, people I see clearly in my mind but haven't spoken with for ages. Those who are now dead. People who inspired me and didn't give up on me when I needed their help; friends and strangers who took me in when I was homeless. I'm grateful to my family and friends for their love and support and to my mother for making it possible for me to attend Kingston University. And to my father for the title, that day on the rocky beach in winter when he was telling me everything he knew about Ansel Adams. I would also like to thank my darling Ute, my sister Ariel, the late Michael Evans, D.B., Alistair Martin, Julien H. and Martin Hennessey for their inspiration.

Insofar as the construction of the novel, it wouldn't be as it is now without the objectivity, ideas, and attention my tutors and fellow students at Kingston University lent, and especially to James Miller for his great insight and support, who continued to advise me into the final stages of the novel. I am very grateful to have had the support of Dodo Ink, and especially Sam Mills – one could not ask for a better editor. I would also like to thank Jessica Craig of Pontas for being an incredible agent.

I would also like to thank Jeremy Narby whose book, *The Cosmic Serpent, DNA and the Origins of Knowledge*, published in 1998 by Jeremy P. Tarcher, Inc., a division of Penguin Putnam, Inc, I've summarized in the novel, and the Penguin Publishing Group who has granted permission to use a quote from Jack Kerouac's *On the Road*. All of Carlos Castaneda's books were a great inspiration, as well as *Magic and Mystery in Tibet* by Alexandra David-Neel published in Great Britain by Souvenir Press, Ltd in 1967. *Fool's Crow: Wisdom and Power* by Thomas E. Mails published in 1991 by Council Oak Books, LLC, in 1991 was a great resource, as well as John G. Neihardt's *Black Elk Speaks* published in 2014 by the Board of Regents of the University of Nebraska.

Dodo Ink would like to thank the following supporters, without whom this book would not have been possible...

Stephen Wright
Jim and Celia Spears
Jonathan Ruppin
Jenny Bullen
The Zebra
Beulah Maud Devaney
Tessa Brechin
Duncan Proudfoot
Françoise Harvey
Marc Owen Jones
Henrik Dahl Jensen
Helen Barrell
Maris Kreizman
Shanshan Xu
Miriam Miller
Victoria Connelly
Sharon Kivland
Blair Rose
ACHUKA
Ian McMillan
Shelley Bowdler
Olivia Bays
Paddy Reynolds
Paul Flieshman
James Miller
Caroline Goldsmith
Aki Schilz

Joseph Bain
Kit Preston Be
Hilary Freeman
James Wise
Kit Caless
Fiona McGlade
Zoe Hayes
Emma Jane Unsworth
Lynda Tahri
Sarah Jones
Andrey Zagoruyko
Tristan Rogers
RP Weston
Alison Ragsdale
Robin and Alison Jones
Dan Martin and Candice Lazarus
David Meller
Chris Williams
Sarah Harkness
Amy Clarke
Andrew Cook
Kat Smith
Ben Pattison-Gordon
Wendy Morrison
Nina Allan
Marion Grace Woolley
Louise Bach
Gabriel Vogt
Rachel Darling
Dixe Wills

Virginia Klein
A J. Ashworth
Sandra James
Jon Day
Thor-Einar Henriksen
Anders Eskemyr
Jennie Gillions
Clive Morrison
Sarah Bradley
Rachel Case
Jacques Testard
Charlie Hill
Jasmin Kirkbride
Hernan Toro
Sarah Wood
Nedda Tichi
Georgina Wright
Francesca R Zerenghi
Emily Sheehan
Jane Greig
Matthew Elizabeth Bryant
Jaimie Batchan
Sofie Blombäck
Alex Herod
Ben Stern
Brendon Warren
David Hebblethwaite
Claire Laurens
Marcus Gipps
Kirstin Lamb

Alice Furse
Philip Berridge
Luke Bartholomew
Dan Coxon
Ana Fletcher
Alison Whittaker
Annabel Gaskell
Naomi Hackett
Marion Kenyon Jones
Tania Hershman
Ben Howkins
Hannah Riches
Arno Vos
Elizabeth Aaron
Susan Osborne
Geoffrey Rabe
Tamara Craiu
Cat Rushmore
Mike Scott Thomson
Helen Swain
Graham Allen
Woody
Brian
James and Paula Wilson
Natalie Marshall
Efford-Eliraz
Nigel Parker
Paul Brindley
Katie Ley
Harriet Devine

Matthew Battle
@Not_James_Brown
Anne Marie Reilly
Adam Banks
Naomi Frisby
Maccewill J.D. Yip
Faaez Samadi
Francesca Ford
Richard Sheehan
Suzanne Kavanagh
Melissa Aho
Literary Kitchen
Ben Fergusson
David Troxler
Matthew Francis
Robert W Archambault
Anonymous
T Hill
Jo Bellamy
Alex Burton-Keeble
Anthony Trevelyan
Stephen Walker
Jayne White
Joanna Robinson
Tze-Wen Chao
Cathryn Steele
Nicholas
Julie Murray (Drynan)
Leesha Gaffney and David Evans
Thomas Sheridan

Irreverence Inc.
Nick Walden
Neil McNally
Jonathan Jones
Lucy Beresford
Ben Spears
Anthony Brown
Amanda Jennings
Russell Heath
Damian Fuller
Kate Williams
Maureen Cuell
Benjamin Spears

About Dodo Ink

At Dodo Ink, we're book lovers first and foremost. From finding a great manuscript to the moment it hits the bookshop shelves, that's how we approach the publishing process at every stage: excited about giving you something we hope you'll love. Good books aren't extinct, and we want to seek out the best literary fiction to bring to you. A great story shouldn't be kept from readers because it's considered difficult to sell or can't be put in a category. When a reader falls in love with something, they tell another reader, and that reader tells another. We think that's the best way of selling a book there is.

Dodo Ink was founded by book lovers, because we believe that it's time for publishing to pull itself back from the brink of extinction and get back to basics: by finding the best literary fiction for people who love to read. Books shouldn't be thought of in terms of sales figures, and neither should you. We approach every step of the process thinking of how we would want a book to be, as a reader, and give it the attention it deserves. When you see our Dodo logo, we'd like you to think of our books as recommendations from one book lover to another. After all, aren't those the ones that we take the greatest pleasure in?

At Dodo Ink, we know that true book lovers are interested in stories regardless of genre or categorisation. That's how we think a publishing company should work, too: by giving the reader what they want to read, not what the industry thinks they should. We look for literary fiction that excites, challenges, and makes us want to share it with the world. From finding a manuscript to designing the cover, Dodo Ink books reflect our passion for reading. We hope that when you pick up one of our titles, you get the same thrill—that's the best thank you we can think of.

www.dodoink.com